VOL. 1, NO. 3   **SUMMER 2018**

FEATURES

NEW STORIES

CLASSIC REPRINT

FROM THE CAT'S PERCH

Welcome to the third issue of *Black Cat Mystery Magazine!*

We recently returned from Malice Domestic, a mystery convention held in the Washington D.C. area each year,) where we had a table in the dealer's room. (Wildside Press also published the convention book, *Mystery Most Geographical*, which we urge to you pick up. It's a lot of fun. John and Carla even has a story in it.)

Reaction there to our first two issues was overwhelmingly favorable, and we had a chance to chat with many of our readers and authors, including Josh Pachter, Barb Goffman, Art Taylor, and many more. Even Michael Bracken (his "Suburbia" starts next page) made the trek from Texas to attend, and he had a great time reminiscing with John about a Pittsburgh writing convention at which they both spoke many years ago.

Funny story: that writer's convention was where John decided to become a mystery writer. He met Linda Landrigan, editor of *Alfred Hitchcock's Mystery Magazine*, and really liked her. Then the convention dinner had an audience-participation mystery play after the meal, and John was the only one at Linda's table to solve it (and she was surrounded by mystery writers). And then on the last day, John won the Mystery Writer's Basket at a raffle. He went home, read 6 months' of back issues of *Alfred Hitchcock's*, wrote three stories in three weeks, and sent them in. Linda Landrigan bought all three. It was Destiny!

Hopefully more of you can attend Malice Domestic next year. Info is at malicedomestic.org.

—John & Carla

Staff

PUBLISHER

John Gregory Betancourt

EDITORS

John Gregory Betancourt

Carla Coupe

WILDSIDE PRESS SUBSCRIPTION SERVICES

Carla Coupe

PRODUCTION TEAM

Sam Cooper

Steve Coupe

Shawn Garrett

Helen McGee

Karl Würf

SUBURBIA

Michael Bracken

Alternating mirror image McMansions, distinguishable only by color schemes and landscaping choices, lined both sides of the subdivision street. Inside one of them, next-door neighbors sat around a card table eating dinner. The hosts—Ken and Joanne—had provided bread and peanut butter; Nick and Cathy had brought a twelve-pack of generic beer and a bag of store-brand potato chips. After they finished, Nick tossed a notice of foreclosure onto the table between them and said, "I received this in today's mail."

As if the notice were somehow contagious, no one touched it. The couple who had lived on the other side of Ken and Joanne remained in their home until the sheriff evicted them. The family on the far side of Nick and Cathy's house had stripped everything of value from their McMansion and then abandoned it. Other empty homes—two of them in the early stages of becoming wildlife refuges—pockmarked the subdivision, their owners victims of the subprime mortgage crisis and their own willingness to overextend themselves while striving to achieve the American dream.

Cathy said, "We wouldn't be in this situation if you hadn't—"

"I bought the house for *you*," Nick said, his voice rising in volume. "You said it was your dream home. Now it's nothing but a nightmare."

To cut short the argument brewing between his neighbors, Ken said, "We won't last much longer. We haven't made a mortgage payment in two months."

"If not for the yard sale," Joanne added as she touched the card table that had replaced their antique dining room table, "we wouldn't have even managed that."

Nick lowered his voice. "We aren't the first and we won't be the last. Everyone thinks we're stupid to try to hold on."

"Maybe we are," Ken said.

"We just need some money."

"We would have money if your brother hadn't—"

Nick spun toward his wife. "That's enough, Cathy!"

But it wasn't. The argument continued until Cathy stormed out of the house crying, Nick close on her heels. The notice of foreclosure remained on the card table, untouched by Ken and Joanne even as they cleaned up the dinner mess.

* * * *

That night Ken and Joanne lay on the air mattress that had replaced their four-poster bed. They had come a long way since the summer they met as pimple-faced teenagers swimming at the abandoned quarry half-way between their hometowns. Everything they had lost, or were about to lose, had come from working hard and pinching pennies. After several minutes of silence, Joanne spoke.

"I stole a loaf of bread today," she said. "I've never stolen anything in my life, but I stole a loaf of bread."

"How—?" Ken started to ask. He had eaten that bread for dinner, and he stopped himself with a shake of his head. "Don't tell me. I don't want to know."

"Have we come to this?" she asked.

Under the covers, Ken took his wife's hand.

"This is tearing apart Nick and Cathy's marriage," Joanne said.

"Not ours," Ken assured her. "Never ours."

Joanne rolled onto her side and rested her cheek on her husband's chest. "Keep telling me that."

* * * *

The stolen loaf of bread provided their toast the following morning. Along with peanut butter and a few potato chips left behind by their neighbors, it also provided lunch and dinner. Ken took a peanut butter sandwich to work with him Monday, leaving the last two slices of bread for Joanne.

As he sat in the park outside his office building unwrapping the sandwich during his lunch break, he watched a mother and daughter digging through the trashcans on the far side of the fountain, eating whatever scraps of food they found. He looked at his peanut butter sandwich and remembered the story of a woman who cried because she had no shoes until she met a man who had no feet. Then he rose, circled the fountain until he reached the woman and her daughter, and handed his lunch to the little girl.

When he told Joanne about it that evening, she asked, "So you haven't eaten anything since breakfast?"

He shook his head.

"All we have is peanut butter and spoons."

"It'll have to do."

Ken filled two glasses with tap water while Joanne retrieved the peanut butter from the pantry and took spoons from the silverware drawer. They carried everything to the card table, where she brushed their neighbors' notice of foreclosure to the floor before they sat together spooning the last of the peanut butter from the jar.

"Friday's payday," Ken said. The car payment would require a significant portion of the money, but they could also pay the electric bill and restock the pantry.

"I don't know if I can last that long."

"We have to."

"I'll walk to the grocery store tomorrow."

"You don't have to do that."

"I have to try," Joanne said. "We have to eat something."

* * * *

Joanne had lost her job at the beginning of the Great Recession, had initially refused to consider any position not equal to the one she lost, and soon found herself overqualified for the few minimum wage jobs that came open. Ken's employer had instituted a ten percent pay cut across the board that allowed every employee to continue drawing a paycheck, but which increased the financial strain many of them faced. Ken and Joanne found themselves draining their savings and retirement accounts, and when their adjustable-rate mortgage interest rate reset at the same time the value of the homes in their subdivision and around much of the country dropped, they found themselves underwater and struggling to remain afloat.

Nick and Cathy had faced similar problems when their mortgage interest rate reset, but Cathy had never worked. She had always been more arm candy than financial contributor, and the sudden increase in household expenses had impacted her worse than any of the others. She'd had to stop her spa treatments, mani-pedis, and regular salon appointments.

Over a beer Friday evening, an hour after learning that his employer had cut everyone back to three-day workweeks, Ken sat with Nick and rehashed everything that had happened during the previous few years, from the highs they felt when they first moved into the subdivision to the constant barrage of telephone calls from debt collectors attempting to milk their dead bank accounts. Ken told Nick about his reduced hours. Nick told him that several middle managers had been let go and that he was certain his number would soon come up.

"I haven't told Cathy yet," Nick said. "She'd only get more upset."

They drank to each other.

"I was telling my brother about our problem," Nick said. "He says he has a solution."

"What's Darnel's big idea?" Ken asked. "Robbing a bank?"

"Better."

Nick's brother had twice been incarcerated for armed robbery, so Ken finished his beer and stood to leave. Nick grabbed Ken's arm and stopped him.

"Darnel's a two-time loser," Ken said. "Why should I listen to anything he has to say?"

"He planned both jobs, and he would have gotten away clean both times if it weren't for his accomplices. One shot his mouth off in a bar. The other was arrested on an unrelated charge and ratted out my brother in a plea deal." Nick lowered his voice. "The two jobs he went down for aren't the only ones he's pulled."

"How much money are we talking?"

"Enough to solve our problems."

"Split how many ways?"

"Five."

Ken pulled his arm free from Nick's grasp. "We won't know any of the other people involved. How can we trust that they'll be any more reliable than the two who flipped on your brother?"

"That's the beauty of this job," Nick said. "The other two people are Joanne and Cathy."

"You want me to involve my wife in an armed robbery?"

"Think about having enough money to keep our homes from being repossessed, enough money to keep us afloat until this recession is over," Nick said. "Besides, they won't do the rough stuff. They'll just drive."

* * * *

Over dinner later that evening, after telling Joanne that he was late because he had stopped for a beer with Nick, Ken told his wife about his reduced work schedule.

"What are we going to do?"

Then he told her what he knew about Darnel's plan.

Joanne shook her head. "No."

"It's no different than stealing bread," he said, "or the pasta you brought home Wednesday."

Joanne stared at him. "I didn't use a gun."

"And you won't have to."

"But you will."

"For show," Ken said. "They have to think we're serious."

Joanne said nothing.

"Will you please listen to what Darnel has to say?"

"What if I don't like his plan?"

"Then we tell them we don't want to be involved."

"Just like that?"

"Just like that."

"And you think they'll let us walk away?"

"I know Nick," Ken said. "If we say we're out, then we're out. No hard feelings."

"I think you're wrong. I think if we listen to the plan then we're committed."

"Look around," Ken said. "How much more do we have to lose?"

"Each other."

* * * *

A few days later Ken and Joanne sat at the dining room table in Nick and Cathy's house, drinking beer and listening as Darnel outlined his plan to rob a check cashing store.

In the middle of the table he had placed a hand-drawn map of the store's layout, showing the location of the safe, the two teller windows made of bulletproof glass, the counter behind the windows and the lobby in front of them. A steel door with a combination lock keypad was the only way into the back room. A steel door that opened from the inside served as an emergency exit, and it opened onto an alley. He indicated the locations of two silent alarm buttons and all the security cameras inside the building. There were none outside.

"The owner and two employees arrive at a quarter to nine. One's a cashier, the other is the muscle. An armored car delivers cash at 9 a.m. Around 9:15, the owner goes to the coffee shop down the street and returns a few minutes later with a large coffee and a Danish in a sack. The store opens at ten," Darnel explained. "On the first and fifteenth, the cash delivery is two to three times that of a regular delivery. On those days, the cash on hand first thing in the morning could be upwards of a quarter million."

Nick whistled. "That'll make a lot of mortgage payments."

"There's a limited window of opportunity," Darnel continued. "When the owner returns with his coffee and Danish, his hands are full. He has to punch in the security code and open the door to the back room without dropping anything. Catch him as he opens the door and you're in."

"What about the two men waiting inside?"

"There will only be one. I'll make sure the muscle has car trouble that morning and is running late. Make the cashier fill the bags. Then zip tie their hands and feet and get the hell out."

Darnel looked at each of them in turn.

"You two do the inside work," he said, pointing to Ken and Nick. Then he pointed to Cathy and Joanne. "One of you remains in the car outside."

"That's three people," Ken said. "Nick said you needed four."

"The fourth is driving the second vehicle."

Ken asked, "Why do we need two cars?"

"When a job like this goes bust, it's often because the driver gets spooked and leaves the inside crew hanging," Darnel explained. "That's why we'll have a backup parked a block away. Both drivers will have burner phones. The second driver will watch everything play out. If the first driver leaves for any reason, the second will pull up and be waiting when you come out."

Darnel continued, explaining how and where they would abandon the getaway vehicles, and how they would divide the money. "You two don't have a pot to piss in, so I'm fronting all the expenses. I get reimbursed for them before we split the take."

"Five ways?" Ken asked.

Darnel nodded.

"And you get twenty percent why?"

"My plan."

"If the plan's foolproof, why don't you do the legwork and take a greater percentage?"

"If I get caught it'll be my third strike," Darnel said.

"I thought you said we wouldn't get caught."

"If you do exactly as I say and keep your mouths shut afterward, you won't."

"Why do you think we can pull this off?"

"The owner's gotten complacent," Darnel explained. "He thinks nobody's stupid enough to knock the place over, and so far they've been right."

Before Ken could ask another question, Joanne excused herself to use the bathroom. She weaved through a black leather living room suite, past a large flat screen television mounted on the brick chimney above the fireplace, and a baby grand piano that neither Nick nor Cathy could play.

While his wife was away, Ken asked, "Why us?"

"No priors. The police will round up all the usual suspects, spread some green among their snitches, and come up short. There's no reason for anyone to be looking at the four of you."

Joanne returned, so Ken finished his beer, stood, and said, "We'll have to think about it."

Darnel grabbed his arm, just as Nick had done in the bar. His grip was much tighter and his voice more commanding. "You're already a part of this."

"But Nick said—"

"Nick told me you were in," Darnel said. "I wouldn't be here if he hadn't."

Ken looked at his wife, but he didn't see her I-told-you-so face. He saw something else and said, "Then we're in."

* * * *

"I know you told me so," Ken said as they crossed the yards from Nick and Cathy's home to their own, "but what was that look about?"

"Cathy has something going on with Nick's brother."

Ken shook his head. "They argue sometimes, but she would never—"

"When I returned from the bathroom, I saw her hand in Darnel's lap."

"Did she see you?"

"She wasn't paying attention to me, so I don't think she knows that I saw what she was doing." Joanne was silent for a moment. Then she asked, "Did you notice anything else?"

"Like what?

"When they came for dinner last week they brought chips and cheap beer. Tonight they served craft beer. Their house might be in foreclosure, but there's not a stick of furniture missing. I don't think they've made any real effort to deal with their situation. I think Nick needs a—a—long pass."

"A Hail Mary."

Joanne nodded. "And Darnel has him convinced this is it."

* * * *

After Darnel made the two men put on latex gloves, he presented them with .38 caliber revolvers.

Nick balked. "Shouldn't we have assault rifles, something that'll make them crap their pants when they see us coming?"

"We're not terrorists," Darnel explained. "We're professionals."

"Speak for yourself," Ken muttered as he examined the .38 he'd been given.

"You want to draw as little attention to yourselves as possible, get in and get out, and for God's sake, don't actually shoot anybody."

"How is a peashooter like this going to frighten anyone?"

Darnel snatched the .38 from Nick's hand, jammed the barrel against the base of his brother's skull and cocked the trigger. Quietly, he asked, "Did you check to see if it was loaded?"

Ken had checked his, and it wasn't.

"Darnel, I—" Nick started.

Darnel squeezed the trigger and the hammer snapped down on an empty chamber.

"Ah, jeez, I almost wet myself."

"That's what we want to the store owner to do when you jam this into the base of his skull."

Nick spun away from his brother. "You made your point."

For the rest of the month, Darnel spent mornings with the two women, teaching them the various routes to and from the check-cashing store, and he spent evenings after work with the two men, rehearsing the robbery in an empty warehouse where he had moved junk around to mimic the interior configuration of the store.

Late each evening, after Ken arrived home from the warehouse, he and Joanne compared what they had learned that day.

"Darnel's thought everything through," Joanne said, "but there could be a hitch in the plan. He spends his afternoons with Cathy, not leaving until it's time to meet you and Nick at the warehouse."

"Why's that a problem?"

Joanne stared at her husband until he realized the implication.

* * * *

Monday, June second, coincided with one of Ken's scheduled off days, and Nick called in sick. They left all forms of identification behind, including jewelry, and pulled on latex gloves before climbing into Darnel's minivan. He drove them to the warehouse where a pair of SUVs waited, both with tinted windows and no identifying decals, parking stickers, or other identifying marks. Each of the women, having flipped a coin, climbed behind the wheel of their assigned vehicle, and each found a burner phone in the center console. Cathy, in the white SUV, would be the first driver, Joanne would be the second, and each phone was prepro-grammed with the number of the other.

The two women had dressed in running shoes, jeans, and T-shirts. They wore a thick layer of make-up, had tucked their hair up under cheap black wigs, and wore large sunglasses. At a glance they looked like other morning commuters—unless someone noticed their latex gloves.

The men—covered from head to toe in jeans, long-sleeve pullover turtleneck shirts, running shoes over knee-high socks, gloves, ski masks, and sunglasses so that no one could see the color of their skin, the color of their hair, or the color of their eyes—climbed into the white SUV with Cathy and two empty canvas duffel bags. They ducked low so they could not be seen by anyone outside the vehicle.

Joanne left the warehouse first. Half an hour later she found an open parking spot a block from the check cashing store. At 9:18 she phoned Cathy's burner phone. "He's left the coffee shop."

The white SUV rounded the corner as the storeowner carried his cof-fee and Danish sack into the lobby of the check-cashing store. The two men were out of the SUV, across the sidewalk, and inside the lobby be-hind the owner as he pulled the steel security door open. Ken pressed the muzzle of his unloaded .38 against the base of the man's skull. He whis-pered in the man's ear, "Don't."

Nick, carrying the duffel bags, pushed past them and caught the lone employee headed for one of the silent alarm buttons. He fired a single shot that lodged in the wall a few inches to the left of the cashier's head. Then he tossed the bags on the desk. "Fill them."

Ken pushed the owner to the floor, zip tied his hands behind his back, and zip tied his ankles. When the duffel bags were full, Nick did the same to the cashier. Then they tucked their revolvers into their waistbands and each carried one of the bags. On the way out, Nick grabbed the sack con-taining the storeowner's Danish.

If anyone noticed two masked men rushing from the check cashing store toting heavy canvas duffel bags, they didn't bother dialing 911, and moments later the white SUV was speeding away with Cathy driving, Nick in the front seat beside his wife, and Ken lying flat on the back seat with the duffel bags.

Almost everything had gone exactly as Darnel had planned.

Nick took off his sunglasses and peeled off his ski mask. As he opened the paper sack from the coffee shop and removed the Danish, he asked, "Did you see the look on that guy's face?"

"What was that all about?" Ken demanded. "The guns weren't supposed to loaded."

Nick didn't answer. Instead, he shoved the Danish in his mouth.

Joanne and Cathy met at a predetermined location on the south side and Ken switched vehicles. A little while later, Joanne parked the black SUV in a public parking garage where they had left their Accord the night before. On the way home, Ken threw his revolver into the river, and they crushed Joanne's burner phone and kicked the pieces into a storm drain. They also disposed of Joanne's wig, Ken's ski mask, and both pairs of sunglasses.

They were home before noon.

Nick and Cathy didn't return until later that afternoon, and Darnel didn't arrive with the money until almost six o'clock.

The five of them sat at the dining room table in Nick and Cathy's home drinking beer, dividing the money, and watching the evening news. The robbery was the lead story on all three local stations, and as they switched from one to another they learned little from any of them that they didn't already know.

Two masked men had robbed the check-cashing store at gunpoint, leaving two employees zip tied on the floor. The store's third employee discovered the robbery when he arrived at work an hour late because his car wouldn't start. An elderly man out for a morning stroll and a woman walking her dog swore they saw a white SUV speeding from the area with a woman behind the wheel. A brief statement from the chief of police indicated that three unidentified suspects had gotten away with at least $200,000, which is what the armored car service had delivered that morning, and that a tip line had been established for any information leading to the arrest and conviction of the three robbers.

When Ken, Joanne, Nick, Cathy, and Darnel finished counting, they realized the actual take was closer to $400,000. Darnel set aside the money to reimburse his expenses and none of the others questioned his accounting methods. Then they divided the rest of the cash five ways.

"What now?" Ken asked.

"Now, nothing," Darnel said. He pointed at Ken and Nick. "Tomorrow you two go to work like always, and you sit on the money until the heat dies down."

"How long will that be?"

"A week, a month, hell it might even be several months."

* * * *

When they returned home, Ken wedged the duffel bag up the chimney and turned to Joanne as she said, "I don't trust Nick. He's reckless and he doesn't like to be told what to do."

"You think he's going to screw this up?"

"He'll do something stupid and we'll have to clean up the mess."

"Then we need to get our stories straight," Ken said. "Where were we this morning and what were we doing?"

They spent the next several hours refining their alibi. They stopped long enough to watch the ten o'clock news, which was a rehash of the evening news, and continued talking until they settled onto the air mattress and fell asleep. Over breakfast, they watched the morning news and learned of a new development. A surveillance camera two blocks from the check cashing store captured a blurry image of a white SUV with a female driver and a male passenger eating a Danish. The police confirmed they were looking for three people, not realizing that five had committed the robbery.

After breakfast, Ken went to work, where break-time conversation about the robbery consumed almost as much of his fellow employees' time as the impending presidential election. He kept his opinions about the robbery to himself but wasn't shy about voicing his support of one presidential candidate over the other.

At lunch, he saw the little girl who had eaten his peanut butter sandwich digging through trashcans with her mother. He handed her that day's lunch—a ham-and-cheese sandwich, chips, and dill pickle spear—and returned to the office without eating.

The next two workdays were much the same, but talk about the robbery had disappeared by Thursday, when other events dominated the news. Every evening Joanne let Ken know that Darnel had spent the afternoon with Cathy, and other than Joanne's keeping track of Darnel's coming and going at their neighbor's house, they avoided Nick and Cathy.

Until Friday afternoon, Ken's other mandatory day off, when they had no choice.

* * * *

Ken opened the door to find Nick on the porch, wild-eyed, smelling of liquor, and waving a .38. Joanne stepped backward into the kitchen when she saw the gun.

"What's wrong?"

Nick pressed the barrel against Ken's chest and backed him into the house. He kicked the door shut. "The sons of bitches fired me today. I came back from lunch to find all my things in a box and a security guard to walk me out."

"You knew that was coming, didn't you?"

Nick continued as if he hadn't heard the question and continued to back Ken up until they stood in the dining room. Ken and Joanne still hadn't picked up their neighbors' notice of foreclosure from the floor and Nick stood on it. "I came home to find my brother in bed with my wife. I'm glad I still had this." He again poked Ken with the revolver's barrel.

"What did you do?"

"They'll never cheat on me again."

"You—?"

Ken didn't finish his question because Nick kept talking.

"I have to leave town, get as far away as possible," he said. "Where's your money?"

"We don't—"

Nick raised his voice. "Don't bullshit me! I want your part of the take and I want it now!"

"Or what?"

"I have two bullets left. First you. Then Joanne."

Joanne stepped out of the kitchen behind Nick, the handle of a cast iron frying pan gripped in both hands like a baseball bat. Nick heard her and spun around. When he did, his shoe slipped on the notice of foreclosure, the bottom of the pan flattened the side of his head, and he fell to the floor unconscious.

"Oh, God," Joanne said as she dropped the frying pan. "What have I done?"

"Nothing worse than what he would have done."

"We've done bad things," Joanne said as Ken gathered her into his arms.

"And we'll do more," he said. "We have to finish this."

* * * *

After Ken calmed his wife, they pulled on latex gloves, removed the key ring from Nick's pocket, and walked outside to find Nick's Lexus parked behind Darnel's minivan. In the back seat were a hastily packed suitcase, a box containing Nick's personal items from his desk at work, and a money-filled duffel bag from the robbery. They looked around. No neighbors lived close enough to see what they were doing, even were they not at work, so Ken carried the bag into their house and shoved it up the chimney with the one already there.

After Ken stuck the notice of foreclosure in Nick's pocket, he and

Joanne carried their neighbor outside and belted him into the passenger seat of his Lexus. At Ken's request, Joanne returned to the house and returned with a plastic trash bag.

Ken moved a half-empty Jim Beam bottle out of the way, slipped behind the wheel of Nick's Lexus, and drove from the subdivision. Joanne followed in their Accord as he drove two hours north of the city, to the quarry where they'd met as teenagers.

He parked the Lexus uphill from the deep end of the quarry. Once they felt certain they were alone—teenagers who frequented the quarry were in school and few other people ever visited it—Ken positioned Nick behind the steering wheel of the car. He wrapped his own arm in a plastic trash bag, put the .38 in Nick's hand, and pressed the muzzle against the underside of his neighbor's chin. Then he turned away and stood as far back as possible as he squeezed the trigger.

Then Ken removed the blood-spattered trash bag from his arm, shifted Nick's car into neutral, and released the parking brake. The Lexus rolled slowly at first, gathered speed, and then went over the edge. It landed top down in the water and sank out of sight.

* * * *

The next day, Joanne called the police. She told them something was wrong at her neighbor's house. An unfamiliar car had been parked in the driveway all night, no one answered when she rang the bell, and the front door was standing open.

The first officer on the scene found the bodies in the bedroom. Before long the subdivision was overrun with police. Ken and Joanne were questioned about their neighbors, repeatedly after the police realized the dead man in the bed had twice served prison time for armed robbery.

Police matched the slugs that killed Darnel and Cathy with one dug from the wall at the check cashing store robbery. They also found a box of .38 cartridges in the garage, six cartridges missing. They knew four had been fired—one into the wall of the store, one into Nick's wife, and two into his brother. When news of the double homicide aired that evening, even before police linked it to the robbery earlier in the week, the owner of Gloria's Guns, Gas, and Grub out by the old highway provided video of Nick purchasing the box of cartridges. A police technician matched photographs of Nick and Cathy with surveillance video of Nick eating a Danish in a speeding white SUV while his wife drove.

Later, they located Darnel's portion of the take in a safe deposit box.

Concluding that Nick, having killed his two accomplices and taken most of the money, was on the run, the police issued a BOLO alert.

After cursory interviews that led the police to believe Ken and Joanne were clueless about their neighbors' activities, they stopped coming around.

* * * *

Ken and Joanne couldn't spend the money, certainly not enough of it to change their situation and draw attention to themselves. So, it dribbled out, just enough at a time that Joanne no longer had to steal bread and pasta. When they finally lost their McMansion, they hardly had any furniture left and were able to squeeze into a one-bedroom efficiency with a large walk-in closet where they stored the duffel bags. Several months later, when the economy turned around, Ken's hours and pay increased to pre-recession levels, and Joanne found a job almost as good as the one she'd lost.

They still have each other, and the money just keeps dribbling out.

Michael Bracken, recipient of the Edward D. Hoch Memorial Golden Derringer Award for lifetime achievement, is author of several books, including *All White Girls*, and more than 1,200 short stories published in *Alfred Hitchcock's Mystery Magazine*, *Ellery Queen's Mystery Magazine*, and many other publications. He lives and writes in Texas.

THE SORORITY HOUSE
Eve Fisher

The Dakota View Apartments are on the south edge of Laskin, below the railroad tracks, with the trailer park directly north, and Nordstrom's Auto to the east. Not exactly your prime location. But south and west is all fields, sweeping to the horizon without a break. That view—soybeans, corn, sunflowers in summer, snow in winter—was why I moved there and why I stay there.

For a long time, it was just me and some retirees. Nice and quiet. But then it changed. And my new neighbors were the last I ever wanted: Jennifer Lundgren and her posse. They were the golden girls of Laskin High, the cheerleaders and Homecoming queens and court, who went to the right colleges and married the right men. Me, I married and divorced Gary Davison—whose family is behind ninety percent of Laskin crime—right out of high school, for God's sake, and they never let me forget it. For years they were safely tucked away in their little subdivision, but now we were all in our thirties, and suddenly they were all "in process" and moved in around me. I couldn't get away from them.

First it was Jennifer. I told myself it was going to be okay, we were all adults now, etc. But:

"Oh, Linda. That's right, you live here, don't you?" "Linda! Would you mind running me over to the Quick Stop before it closes?" "So, Linda. Dating anybody these days?" "Linda… seriously, cargo pants?" "Oh. Linda. Did Gary every get out of prison? Really?" "Oh, Linda…"

It didn't help that she'd hooked up with Tim Rosholt. Big mistake, in my book. Tim's been a player since day one, and why she thought he'd change, I don't know. He didn't. He was still putting the moves on every woman in sight. I fended him off in the laundry room, in the parking lot, once in the hallway. But Jennifer seemed oblivious, even though she'd torn Dave a new one every time she thought he even looked at another woman.

The end of June, Ellen Corson had a big fight with Steve, nothing unusual there. But this time she moved out and in with Jennifer, and then got a place of her own, across the hall from me. The parties got bigger, louder, longer, and now there were two apartments for folks to weave between, both on my floor.

The week after July Fourth, Calla Holter suddenly showed up. I remember I came home and found her, sitting on the steps like a little rabbit with that twitching nose, waiting for Ellen to come home and take her in, which Ellen did. When Ellen booted her out a month later, to her own apartment downstairs, Calla had somehow transformed herself into a freeze-dried hippie in long skirts, sandals, tank top, unshaven armpits and no bra. Ellen said, disgustedly, that Calla had gone completely mental. Grant Tripp—who'd thought I was exaggerating about all of it—saw her at Art in the Park, dancing alone barefoot on the grass, and asked what drugs she was on. I told him, "You're the cop. Ask her."

Now Calla would typically have been town topic number one for weeks. But then Mandy Fisk not only left Brian and moved in with Jennifer, *but* she was gone within days to join her true love, Susan what's-her-face, the woman who'd come up from Denver over the winter to research country records of women pioneers in the 1800's.

Jennifer was flabbergasted. Mandy had been her best friend for years, and she swore she'd never dreamed that Mandy was "that way." Calla seemed a bit envious. Ellen was, as always, snide. I was surprised, but not that much. I work at the courthouse, and I've seen a lot. I was only sorry that Mandy—who'd asked me one day in the laundry room to meet her for a drink at Mellette's Lounge—never showed. I'd have loved to hear *that* story from the horse's mouth.

Lisa Johnson was just the icing on the cake. Five women in one summer: people were saying it must be in the water. What I knew was that Dakota View had been turned into a sorority house. The doors were always open, the music loud and constant, and they were always running from apartment to apartment, including mine, for matches, groceries, gossip, rides, you name it. And it was only going to get worse.

Meanwhile, the soon-to-be ex-husbands had their own ways of coping. Dave Lundberg had transferred all his dating activity to Sioux Falls. Steve Corson came to a couple of the parties, where he looked like a dog eyeing a steak on the kitchen counter. Morten Holter was fighting Calla over everything about their coming divorce, and came over regularly to shout the place down, especially when Calla announced that she was going back to school to get her Ph.D. in something or other (my guess: driving Morten crazy). As for poor Brian Fisk, nobody ever saw him, but rumor was he was drinking heavily every night, alone, with the lights out, and who could blame him? He must have been completely humiliated. And Bob Johnson cruised our building regularly, sometimes sitting outside for hours. Did I mention Bob was a policeman? No matter what time of the day or night, there he was, in his car, smoking a cigarette and watching us. Very unnerving.

And then, a week after Lisa moved in, Mandy Fisk's beaten body was found, in one of the dumpsters outside Cortland Construction. Earl Olson had been dumpster diving for God knows what, and the smell had about knocked him out. He'd complained to Cortland, who'd looked deeper, and called the police.

"Do you think they've arrested him yet?" Calla asked. The Saturday morning mail had arrived, and for once we were all at the mailboxes downstairs.

"Who?" Jennifer asked. She looked awful.

"Brian Fisk, who else?"

"Oh, my God," Jennifer moaned. "Brian… He must have…"

"Maybe," I said. "Anyway, we know she didn't run off with Susan."

"But she wrote that wonderful note!" Calla wailed.

"Maybe not," I said. Everyone looked at me. "Maybe it's a forgery." I looked over at Jennifer, who had turned green. "You still got it?"

"No."

"I have it," Calla said. We all stared at her. "It was so beautiful, I hated to throw it out…"

"Well, you'd better dig it out now, because the police are going to want to see it," I told her.

"Oh. Of course. Of *course*." She ran into her apartment.

"She kept it?" Jennifer exclaimed. "Is she nuts?"

"What have I been telling you?" Ellen replied.

"Oh, who cares?" Jennifer snapped. "Mandy's dead. I never dreamed… She said he got violent when he was drunk, but I…" She clutched her stomach. "I think I'm going to be sick."

Ellen put her arm around Jennifer. "Come on upstairs, Jen. You need to lie down."

The two of them went upstairs. I stayed put and lit a cigarette. It was a damned good idea: kill your wife and make it look like she's just one more in a string of runaway wives. I'd never thought Brian was that clever.

Calla came back out in the hallway, flushed, note in hand. "Where'd everybody go?"

"Upstairs. Jennifer was going to be sick," I said. "That it?"

It was a plain piece of faded white paper, like from one of those pads in the back of the dime store, written in black ink.

I'm off to Susan's. God, I love that girl. We're going to have a blast! Colorado is my spiritual home. I'm probably never going to come back, and if I do, I'm crazy! Love, Mandy.

I remembered reading it before. Jennifer had accepted it as genuine. So had Brian killed her on her way to meet Susan? Or was it a forgery? And if so, when had Brian been in the building? Why didn't any of us remember seeing him?

"Can I have it back?" Calla asked.

I looked down at the note. I'd been rubbing the edge of it—a corner had been torn off the top—under my thumbnail while I thought. "Sure."

"Do you remember Susan?"

"Kind of. I wonder... did she leave... When Mandy left, was it really to hook up with Susan, or just get away from us all?"

"I'm sure she wanted to get away from Tim," Calla said bitterly. "He hasn't changed a bit, you know. Mr. Grab 'Em and Grope 'Em. They're talking about moving to Sioux Falls. He's not going to change there, either. I warned Jennifer about him, but she just laughed at me... I to warn Mandy, but... I thought we had something special..." She moved her hands as if she was rubbing a volleyball.

"Are you coming out to me, Calla?"

Calla blushed, but I wasn't sure it was from embarrassment. "What was Susan like?"

"Does it matter? Mandy didn't run off with her."

Calla bent her head. "That's right. I've got to remember that. But who..." The intensity of her voice worried me.

"Do you remember seeing Brian around the night Mandy disappeared?" I asked.

"No." Calla looked up at me. "I don't remember anything. I was out like a light." I nodded. Her tone became confidential. "Truth is, I'd asked Mandy to move in with me, and she said no. I didn't take it well. A bottle of wine and a few..."

A car door slammed outside, and we turned to see Grant Tripp and Jim McKinney coming up the sidewalk.

"You'd better tell them everything," I said, and went upstairs.

* * * *

There was no party that night at Dakota View. I didn't have a date, so I made a TV dinner and turned on the TV. I was brooding because Grant had sent Jim McKinney to take my statement. Was it because he and I were semi-interested, or because we semi-worked together, or because I was a semi-suspect? Or, worst of all, because my testimony didn't matter? Who questioned Brian Fisk? Probably Detective Jonasson himself. Had Brian sobered up? Did he have an alibi? Had he broken down and confessed? And there was poor crazy Calla—

There was a knock at the door.

Tim Rosholt stood there, a worried look on that excessively handsome face. "Linda? Listen, can you come next door? Jennifer's semi-hysterical and she needs to talk to someone who knows about legal stuff."

"What happened?"

Tim spread her hands wide. "I… Just come, okay?"

Well, I'd eaten, so I went.

Jennifer was curled up on her sofa, drinking scotch.

"Oh, thank God," Jennifer said, when she saw me. "Listen, I've got to know what's going on. Grant and Jim… Do you know they say Brian has an *alibi*?"

"Really? Did they tell you what it was?"

"He was already in jail!"

Jennifer waved at Tim, who continued the story: "DUI. Down in Sioux Falls. Nobody to bail him out, he was broke, they kept him till the next morning."

"I just don't believe it," Jennifer said. "And then they asked me a ton of questions. And they wanted to search my apartment!"

"Well, that makes sense. Did they?"

"No! Why should they?"

"Because… Look, Mandy was killed," I explained. "And she either was on her way to this Susan in Colorado, or she wasn't. Now if she was, then she would have packed up everything. But, if she wasn't, if that note was a forgery, or a lie or something, then what happened to all her stuff?"

"That damned dumpster, where else?" Jennifer snapped.

"*All* of it?" Jennifer stared at me as if I were teaching quantum physics. "Jen, they're looking for evidence, and your place was the last place she was seen alive. So of course they want to search. They're going to search. With your cooperation or without it."

"Oh." Jennifer over at Tim. "So, either she packed up everything and took it away, or she didn't, and somebody else did."

"Exactly," I congratulated her.

"Wow. You want a drink?" I shook my head. "Really? How about some herbal tea? Make her some of that acai tea, Tim." I tried not to make a face. I hate that stuff. "So you're saying that somebody… Oh, my God. Somebody came in… Brian. No, Brian has that alibi. But someone came into my apartment…"

"If—" I heard the beeping of a microwave.

"And got all her stuff and…" Jennifer leaped up, cell phone in hand, nearly knocking over the lamp beside her.

"Who are you calling?" Tim asked, coming back from the kitchen. He handed me a cup of lukewarm tea. I smiled and took a sip. It was awful, especially since he'd piled the sugar in.

"The police, of course. To let them know they can come and look all they want."

"Call them in the morning," I suggested. "Right now all you'll get is the dispatcher."

"It's a murder case. Surely somebody will be there."

"You've been watching too much TV."

Jennifer clicked her phone shut and sat back down heavily. "This is so unfair. Drink up. I wonder who… I'll bet it was that bitch, Lisa."

"*Lisa*?"

"Yes, Lisa. She had the gall to tell me that Tim was screwing around with Mandy. More like she was screwing around with Brian, if you ask me. She's always been a little slut. Either way, she had a down on Mandy, and I'll bet she and Brian worked this whole thing out." I glanced over at Tim, who was biting his lip. "They probably worked it all out, even to Brian's perfect alibi…" I suppose I was looking skeptical. "Well, how else could they have done it? Who else could get in my apartment?"

"Anybody," I said. "My God, the doors are never locked in this place."

"No, but Tim or I are always around. One of us would have noticed a stranger. But Lisa…"

"But Lisa wasn't even here yet," I pointed out. "She didn't move in with Ellen until after Mandy left. Was killed. I'll bet she's got an alibi, too. Fighting with Bob, if nothing else."

Jennifer swallowed, looked at Tim, then back at me. "Oh."

"Alibis matter, Jen," I said.

"I know that. Grant asked us all where we were that night."

"And could you remember?"

"We were at Ellen's party, right, Tim?"

"Right."

"Along with everybody else," I commented.

"You weren't." Tim's eyes wandered from my chest to my face and back again.

"No. I was up in Sisseton at the Stark family reunion. Almost as excit-ing, what with Aunt Matt in full force."

Jennifer jumped up, knocking my tea all over the coffee table, and cried, "I just saw her—remember seeing her. Mandy. That night. It was the last time I saw her dancing, at Ellen's. And then she left… I thought she'd just run over here to get a Tampax or something… But she was gone… Calla." Jennifer sat up and blew her nose loudly. "I've got to talk to Calla. Maybe she saw something."

"Doubtful," I said. "She was passed out in her apartment. Listen, I need to—"

"In her apartment? How do you know?"

"She told me. She'd had a disappointment and drowned her sorrows." I had no intention of telling them what the disappointment was. Calla got enough ridicule.

"Oh." Jennifer got up, swaying on her feet. "I need to use the bathroom." She staggered off.

"She okay?" I asked.

Tim shrugged. "She's been having a hard time—"

There was a crash and a thud from the bathroom that brought us racing in. Jennifer was lying on the bathroom floor, bathroom products scattered around her. She looked up at us and said, "I don't feel so good."

"Come on, honey," Tim said. "I'll put you to bed."

"No. I don't want to. I'm scared. I don't want to be alone."

"I'm not going anywhere, sweetheart," Tim said. "I'm right here with you."

I stepped back as Tim lifted her up and carried her into the bedroom, her red hair spilling all over his arm just like on the cover of those romance novels Jennifer bought by the pound.

"She's out like a light." Tim's eyes fixed on my chest again.

"Good. I'd better go home."

"Oh. Do you have to? I mean, we could have a glass of wine together…"

"No thanks. Not tonight. I'm wiped out."

"Oh, come on. You sure?"

"Yes," I said firmly.

"Okay. Well, thanks for coming."

"I don't know that I helped…"

"Well, you're the one who knew that there wasn't anybody at the cop shop."

"Glad to be of service," I said, and ducked out.

The phone was ringing when I walked into my apartment. It was Grant.

"Listen, I'm finally off duty and down here at the Norseman's. If you'd care to join me, I'll buy you a beer and fill you in on the gossip."

"I already heard about Brian's alibi," I replied.

"That was quick."

"It's the sorority house. Gossip travels fast."

"Sounds like it. So, you coming down?" Grant asked.

"Sure."

I hoped I didn't sound too eager. And it took me a shamefully short time to get down there, considering we weren't dating or anything.

"So, what's this juicy gossip?" I asked.

"Lisa has gone back home to Bob."

"Really? When?"

"About an hour ago. Down at the station. She had suitcases with. Cried all over him. He enjoyed it, but I think she enjoyed it more."

"She always was a drama queen. You should have seen her in high school."

"No, thanks."

"Of course, the question is, who's going to move in with Ellen now?"

He leaned back and grinned at me. "My bet is nobody. Ellen is moving in with Ward Powell."

My jaw dropped: Ward Powell was our state's attorney. "That could be a major conflict of interest if it turns out she killed Mandy."

"Yeah. Well, listen, speaking of that, you need to start being more careful over there. Someone beat that woman's head in. Keep an eye out when you go in or out. Make sure you keep your keys in your hand. They'll give you an extra punch if you need it."

"Thanks for making me feel so safe," I snarled, mostly because I'd been thinking the same thing.

"I don't want you to feel safe," he snapped back. "I want you to be safe. Those apartments are way out on the edge of town, and who knows—it might be a stranger that killed Mandy."

I thought of Calla's face when she said, "I'd asked her to move in with me…"

"And call me if anything happens. Anything at all." I suppose I looked mulish, because he said, "I mean it, Linda."

"Okay, okay. Now can we change the subject? To something that might let me sleep tonight?"

I got home at ten thirty (Grant had morning shift, and I had church), and the building was as dark as it used to be before the girls moved in. I was quiet as a mouse walking in, careful not to slam the door, not to wake anyone up, my keys tight in my fist. I was starting up the stairs when I heard a familiar door. Calla had heard me. I stepped into the shadows, hoping to be invisible, and saw a spray of red hair falling out of Calla's door.

I almost said, Jennifer? But I didn't want to deal with her, either. But as I darted up the stairs I couldn't help but wonder what was she doing in Calla's apartment? She'd been passed out cold barely an hour ago. You couldn't sober up that quickly. Unless…

I had my key in the lock, my hand on the knob, when I turned around and saw Tim peering out of their door. I saw that tea cup spilling all over the coffee table, right after I'd said—what was it? That I'd been out of town that night. By now Tim was staring at me, and I could hear footsteps coming up the stairs. I dove into my apartment, slammed the door shut behind me and locked it. The bitch had been pumping me for information. And I'd given her exactly what she'd been looking for. Someone without an alibi.

I pulled out my cell phone and hit speed dial.

Grant answered. "Hello?"

"Grant, it's Linda. Listen, there's something weird going on over here, and I think somebody better come and check on Calla fast. I'm not sure, but I think she might be drugged."

"Suicide?"

"No. Attempted murder. But it's going to be set up to look like—"

I jumped as someone knocked on my door.

"Linda?" Jennifer.

"Please," I hissed urgently into the cell phone. "Come quickly."

"Linda, I need to talk to you." Jennifer's voice sounded a bit urgent itself.

"I'm on my way," Grant said. "Leave your cell phone on. I'm forwarding your call to dispatch."

"I'm tired, Jennifer!" I called back.

"Linda! I just need to talk to you."

"I'm just trying to stay safe, Jen. I know what happened." There was silence. "Mandy slept with Tim, didn't she? And you caught her? What happened? You catch them in mid-banging? And bashed her head in? And Tim did such a terrible job of disposing her body?" I was sounding like I was still in high school, everything ending in a question, but I couldn't stop it. "And so you needed someone to take the rap? And Brian had an alibi—"

I screamed at that point, because something heavy rocked against my door. My bet was Tim. He was big, it wasn't that good a door, he could break in. I ran back into my kitchen. A baseball bat. The door rocked again. I didn't have a baseball bat. Again. A knife. The frying pan. Where was Grant?

I took the frying pan in both hands and went over to the door, ready to whack it down on whoever's head made it through. The door shook again, and so did my arms. And then it stopped. I could hear voices, one of them I was pretty sure was Grant's. There was a commotion that I couldn't interpret from inside. And then, finally, a knock.

"Linda? It's Grant. Are you all right?"

I opened the door, and he pulled me into a hug that nearly strangled me.

They got Calla to the hospital and pumped her stomach out. She was fine, except for the aftereffects and the knowledge that her high school friend tried to kill her. Jennifer tried to bluff her way out—she'd never known a situation she couldn't talk her way out of—but Tim collapsed. Tim had forged the note for her, flattered to think that a woman would kill over him.

As for me, I'm thankful that Dakota View's getting back to normal. Jennifer's apartment was quickly rented by Vern and Viola Torgeir, both in their seventies. Two more retirees are coming soon, since Ellen did move in with Ward, and Calla decided she needed to get back to nature and moved to Colorado. Really. She moved to Boulder and has an apartment downtown. This time, we checked.

✗

Eve Fisher has had almost thirty stories published in *Alfred Hitchcock Mystery Magazine*, as well as science fiction, poetry, and plays. She contributes to the mystery writers' blog, SleuthSayers, (www.sleuthsayers.org), and her website is www.eve-fishermysteries.wikispaces.com. She lives in South Dakota with her husband and 5,000 books.

TOURIST SEASON

JM Taylor

I told Sylvia we should have come earlier, when the restaurant wouldn't be so loud, but she said she was too young for early-bird specials.

"You're seventy-nine," I told her. "And I'm eighty-two. If we wait much longer, we'll be feeding the worms those early birds eat."

But Sylvia is the one who drives—I had to give up my license when the glaucoma got too thick—and she decides when and where we go, so I have to put up with her foolish choices if I want a night out.

I was waiting on the veranda when she pulled up in her husband's Mercury Sable. I've been telling her for twenty years it's time to get a new car, but she won't listen. She says it was in his will that she keep it, but I think she's just being difficult. I tell you, that man had a new car, always a Mercury, every year. He wouldn't expect her to hold on to that jalopy this long, and don't tell me Abe Foster didn't leave his wife more than well-provided for, though you won't see more than a couple hundred in her bank account. Still, she insists. Sylvia's always been making up lies, just to get my goat.

Like that time when we were in high school. I was a year ahead of her, and the president of the Amanuensis Club. She was the treasurer, but she already had her eyes set on a bigger prize. Stanley Cassel was a senior. Last year, he pitched our school's only championship game. He was handsome and popular and dumb as a barnacle. We were all in love with him.

Stanley was being recruited by some of the minor league teams, and Sylvia decided to interview him for the school paper. She wore her best skirt and her tightest sweater and offered to meet him on the bleachers in the outfield after practice. Now, I'm not saying that she made up the entire article as a breathless piece of fiction, to cover the fact that several people saw them necking behind the equipment shed. But Stanley couldn't put two sentences together with a roll of tape, and she made him out to be as eloquent as the president.

You'd think that was the end of the story, that Sylvia used her position to get Stanley Cassel's famous hands under that tight sweater of hers, but there's more. Something about that interview made Stanley her puppy dog. He even came to our meetings. He said it was to be near his Sylvie, and she clearly encouraged the attention. Maybe.

But just before graduation, when he had a deal to join a team down in North Carolina, the club's dues fund was pilfered. Sylvia's key, which she always kept around her neck (next to Stanley's ring) was gone. Her ledger proved all the money should have been in the lock box, but it was empty, except for a smudge on the lock. It was rosin, the same stuff he used when he was pitching. No one wanted to call the police, but Stanley lost his pitching deal, and he never showed up to graduation. He left town, and no one ever heard from him again. Sylvia was heartbroken, and maybe that's why she suddenly had herself a dress that looked just like the one Grace Kelly wore in *Rear Window*. Maybe.

Even now, when I try to ask her about that dress, and what Stanley had to do with the money, all she ever says is that he was a crumb for doing *that* to her. I've never been able to figure out if "that" was stealing the money, wanting to leave her to play baseball, or whatever it was that she let him do behind the equipment shed. I'm certain, though, that she pinned the whole thing on poor Stanley, and he was too stupid to figure out how he lost everything before he graduated high school.

Anyhow, there we were at Captain Sutton's Table. It's right next to the boatyard, been there since my kids were little. The food's not great, but it's got a perfect view of the harbor and all the tourists come here. They make a strong cocktail, too. I thought we'd have trouble getting a seat, but Sylvia just said, "Don't be a worry wart," and strolled into the foyer.

The hostess was new, the school year just finished. She was a little slip of a girl, younger than we were when Stanley had his hat and mitt handed to him. About my grandson's age, so they probably go to school together. The town's got only the one high school, though it's a different building than the one me and Sylvia went to. They turned our school into a retirement home. Thank goodness we're both still strong enough to live in our own houses. I'd hate to go back to that old gothic castle for anything, especially to wait to die. I mean, isn't that what high school is for, anyhow?

The little girl smiled but said that it would be a ten minute wait. Sylvia nodded, said, "That's fine." Then she turned to me, and said loudly, "She says ten minutes. You can handle that, Kate, right?"

I screwed up my eyes and leaned on her shoulder. "What's that?"

"Ten minutes!"

"Ohh, I guess," I said. I leaned a little harder on Sylvia's shoulder.

The slip looked worried and said, "I'll see if I can make it faster." She scuttled into the dining room, her head turning back and forth like a lighthouse.

About a minute later, she came back with a triumphant smile on her face. She grabbed a couple of laminated menus and sashayed us to a table in the middle of the room. The bus boy was still cleaning it off, but at least we were able to sit down. She even took our drink orders, while our waitress stood by, huffing. Sylvia got a glass of white wine. I got a Bloody Mary, heavy on the horseradish, heavy on the vodka. I don't drive.

The July Fourth holiday was coming later in the week, and the room was packed with folks from away. Men in brand new polo shirts with bright matching colors. Little boys with their hair slicked down, wives and daughters in stiff sundresses and bright jewelry. They laughed loudly, making sure everyone knew they were having a good time. Just perfect American families out for a wholesome meal.

Now the townsfolk in work clothes huddled over their plates, intent on moving on to the next day. If they talked, they spoke in half sentences, with the rest to be filled in with twitchy eyes and gritted teeth.

When the table was cleared and the drinks and our waters arrived, I told Sylvia, "My son called yesterday. He's taking a new job."

"Didn't he just start a new job about half a year ago?" She didn't have to yell, because my hearing is every bit as good as hers.

"Sent all those jobs to Mexico or something. Besides, this new one's got health insurance. He's still trying to pay off my daughter-in-law's hospital bills."

"It's a damn shame. But she shouldn't have been riding a bike at her age. They make cars for grown-ups, you know." Sylvia always had that practical side to her.

I was about to ask her about her own daughter, who was trying to find herself out west, but this tourist started hacking up a lung at the next table. I looked over. One of those picture-perfect families with pale skin and bright clothes. I turned back to Sylvia and said, "What's new from Santa Fe?"

"Margaret? She gave up on yoga. Moved to Colorado. Says it's the clean mountain air, but I think it's because they legalized…"

I didn't hear anything else. The lady at the next table was barking like a seal again. The rest of them, her husband and their two kids, pretended they didn't hear anything. I leaned over with my glass of water. "Drink this," I said. "It's got lemon in it."

The woman took it and thanked me, but they looked at us like no one had ever done a good deed for them before. I saw her lean over and whisper something to her husband. Probably asking him if he thought I'd poisoned her. The little boy said loudly for all of us to hear, "Mom, what did you say?" and she hushed him. She looked at me one more time, held back another spasm, and then lifted the glass to me like a toast.

Our waitress Molly came by and said hello. We recognized each other from past years. I ordered fried haddock, even though I knew it was over-priced, and Sylvia got the chicken parm. It was only after that that Sylvia said to me, "I forgot my wallet."

I rolled my eyes. Now I'd have to take care of the bill. On a fixed income. "How could you? You had it on your lap the whole time you were driving. Do you think I'm going to steal from you right there in the car?" She shrugged, and I looked around the room again. No one of any interest, so I turned back to the coughing lady. Her face was red, but she was mostly quiet.

"The lemon helped, didn't it?" I said.

"Yes, thank you," she replied. "It was very nice of you."

"Don't think anything of it," I told her. "I've raised six children with two husbands, have eight grandchildren, and one great-grand-daughter. I'm eighty-two years old, so I know how to handle a cough."

The children looked like they wanted to crawl away and die. I understood. The husband gulped his beer and said, "You look twenty years younger than that. What's your secret?"

"At least one of these every day." I held up my Bloody Mary and sipped it through the straw. I winked at the little boy, who cringed. Who was this crazy lady talking to his reserved city parents?

"Well, it was really nice of you," the woman said.

She turned back to her kids, but before she could speak, I said, "My name is Kate, and this is Sylvia. We've known each other since grammar school." I leaned towards the little girl, who looked about eight. "Did you ever read about one-room school houses? We went to one until seventh grade. I was a year ahead of Sylvia, but we sat next to each other for years. What do you think of that?"

The little girl looked to her mother for guidance, then said, "Sounds weird."

I laughed. "You here visiting? Where are you from?"

The man said they were from somewhere in Ohio. "It's a blue-collar town," he said. "Like this. But not as nice." He managed to insult both our towns in one sentence.

"Quaint," the woman added with a smile, as if it was a compliment. Third time's the charm.

"My family settled this town," Sylvia added.

"Imagine," the husband said. "You must be like royalty here." I'm sure his mother taught him never to ignore someone else's comment. Or maybe his father taught him to always have the last word. Either way, I barreled on.

"She is royalty. Her husband practically ran this town for forty years." I didn't say that he was the son of a bootlegger who made all his money smuggling Canadian whiskey on his fishing boat.

"Isn't that nice," the woman said, looking toward the kitchen for their food. But ours came first. Sylvia started right in while I talked.

"He founded the hospital and always made sure the police department had the latest equipment." *They had to, if they had any hope of catching up with him. They never did.* "Now, my own first husband, Harry, he was a fisherman. Had traps covering half the bay here. I had my first two with him. One's in Portland working in a law office, the other is with her father."

The man blinked twice, and the woman went pale. "What happened?" he said.

"With Harry? They found him shot in his trawler. Police said it was probably a dispute over the traps. They found three already in the boat with him, empty. The rest were trailing behind like an anchor. Never did find the culprit."

"That's horrible," the woman breathed. I could barely hear her over the noise of the restaurant, but I could read in her face the horror of a ruined vacation dinner. Their food came, but she kept her eyes on me. The kids stole her French fries. Enterprising youth.

"And I guess I have to ask," the man started.

"About her daughter," Sylvia said. She always needs to insert herself. "Six years old. Measles, you know."

"It seemed to start as a cold," I said. I pointed to the glass of water. "Drink up, sweetie," I told the woman. "I'm sure yours is just allergies or something, but still, the citrus will help."

She drank half of it in a gulp. The kids were eating, ignoring us, but the parents had forgotten them. Not one to leave the moment hanging, Sylvia piped up.

"That's going back a long time," she said. "Medicine's gotten better since then, of course. And in the sixties not every house in town had electricity, let alone televisions. But we had one of the first color sets in the state. Now, what you really want to know is about Kate's second husband."

"What was he like?" the woman asked.

"A movie star," Sylvia said.

"He made television commercials," I corrected. "Local ones. For fish restaurants and banks and car dealerships."

"Did he ever really make a movie?" the little girl asked.

"Not the kind you'd see," Sylvia said with a wink. Mom gulped, and dad tried to hide a grin.

Before Sylvia could talk about those early banned-in-Boston films, I jumped in and said, "It wasn't like that, though. Not really. Frank really was just a local ham. I met him about a year after Harry was killed. I was taking Garreth, the one who now works as a title examiner for that lawyer in Portland, to the doctor. I was a single mother of one by that time, with no family and every little thing had me worried. You know how it is, right?"

They nodded.

"Anyhow, Frank was making a commercial at the diner. They had the big lights set up, and screens, and huge cameras. He was so handsome. Garreth wanted to see how they made the commercials, so we watched a little while. When they took a break, the boy asked for Frank's autograph. The nerve! Anyhow, Frank signed a napkin for him, then gave me his own number. I didn't think someone like him, someone we saw every night selling hardware or ice cream, would want to step out with a single mother, but he was so kind. We had four more kids before it ended."

"He died, too?" the woman asked.

"I wouldn't know," I said, finishing the Bloody Mary. "One night he said he got a role in a national commercial in New York. He said he'd be gone just a week." I looked at the parents, studying their ages. "You probably saw it, that ad for the mouthwash, with the germs in the man's mouth?"

"I loved that commercial!" the man said. "The guy's looking in the mirror, and they zoom in and you see the germs dressed as construction workers. Was your husband the man looking in the mirror?"

"No, dear. He was the germ with the blue hard hat. Anyhow, it made him quite a bit of money, and he sent some of it home. Same with the money from the next few spots, too. But he never came back. Sometimes I catch sight of him in those late-night commercials for folding canes, but I think they've been running those for ten years now, so who knows what he's up to?"

Their waitress, a new girl this summer, came by to check on their food. I saw the woman whisper something and the waitress looked our way and nodded.

I smiled and said, "Anyhow, we made do. I worked as a bookkeeper at the quarry, even before I met Frank. All of my kids went to college or trade school. Well, the ones who made it to adulthood. But I should let you eat. Look at me, gabbing away while your food gets cold."

"She always did have the gift of gab," Sylvia said with a laugh.

When our waitress came by, we each ordered another drink. I still hadn't touched my fried haddock. When I did finally start to eat, it gave them permission to focus on their own food. The kids were asking about dessert. The father was about to say yes, but the mom jumped in. She said something quiet to her husband, who nodded. They both finished eating quickly and called for the check.

"How's your chicken?" I asked Sylvia.

"Not as good as last year. I wonder if they have a new cook?"

They family got up to leave. As they passed our table, the woman said, "It was really very nice talking to you. I can't wait to explore your town."

"Enjoy the rest of your dinner," the man said. They left, the kids grumbling about their missed dessert.

When they'd gone, their waitress told us, "That family you were talking to? They paid your check, can you believe it? Isn't that nice?"

"You're darn right it's nice," our waitress Molly told her as she delivered our second round. "Usually, these two con artists only get their drinks paid for. See you ladies tomorrow night?"

✗

JM Taylor lives in Boston with his wife and son. He's appeared in *Tough*, *Crime Syndicate*, *Mystery Weekly*, and *Thuglit*, among others. *Spinetingler* named his novel *Night of the Furies* one of 2013's best. Follow him on Twitter at @taylorjm7 and like his Facebook page *Night of the Furies*.

DIVERSIONS
John M. Floyd

Dave Carson woke up in a bed in a small room with bare walls and a wooden floor. A young woman with curly red hair and a Winchester rifle across her lap sat watching him from the room's only chair, which was leaning against one of the two doors. Through a window beside the door he saw a swatch of blue sky so bright it hurt his eyes. Squinting, Carson sat up in the bed and groaned: his head hurt, too, and his wrists were tied together. With a probing finger he touched the knot above his right ear, and when he did he remembered what had happened.

"Somebody hit me," he said. "From behind."

"Not me." The woman, who wore a shiny five-pointed star on her shirt, shifted in her chair. "I heard it was the bank manager. Luckett."

Carson nodded. "Skinny guy, squirrely-looking?"

"That's him." She cocked her head a bit, as if to better examine his face. "Do you know why you're here?"

"Because I robbed the bank, I guess."

"Actually, you *tried* to rob the bank."

How true, Carson thought. And a poor try it was. But he'd followed the plan, and had done exactly what he'd been told...

That, of course, was the problem. He should never have listened to Barnes.

He also wasn't listening now. The woman had said something more, and he'd missed it.

"Excuse me?" he said to her.

"I said, 'But that wasn't what I meant.' We both know you've been arrested. I meant 'Do you know why you're *here*?'" She glanced around at the almost-empty room. "In this place."

Suddenly another image flashed through his mind. He remembered the BOOM of the explosion, just after the sheriff had arrived in the bank lobby this morning and had forced him to drop his gun, and just before he'd been knocked out. Carson recalled flinching at the sound of the blast, like everyone else, and turning to stare out the tall windows that framed the front door, and at the gray-black smoke pouring from the building on the other side of the street.

"I guess that explosion we heard… the jail was over there, wasn't it? Did somebody blow up the jail?"

"Most of it. Welcome to our temporary detention facility."

Carson looked around at the stark walls, the glass window, the two doors, and noticed for the first time the sharp but pleasant smell of new wood. His boots, he saw, were in the corner beside the bed. "What *is* this place?"

"An extra room, behind the sheriff's house. He was planning to rent it out."

"How long have I been here?" he asked.

"About an hour."

"I don't see any bars. What's keeping me in?"

"I am." She lifted the rifle off her lap, then lowered it again.

Despite the situation, he felt himself smile. "Will we be spending the night together?"

She didn't smile back, but her face softened a bit. "I doubt it. Sheriff Ward'll be back in a minute. He wants to talk to you."

"I bet he does. How'd I get to this fake jailhouse?"

"The folks at the bank carried you here when we found out about the damage to the real jail. If it'd been up to them I think they'd have hanged you instead."

"For pointing a gun at 'em?"

"People been hanged for less."

"Indeed they have," he said. "And who might you be?"

"I might be Deputy Morton."

He studied her a moment. "You a real deputy?"

"This month I am." She tapped her star. "This is my uncle's badge—he's home with a broken leg."

"An interim jail and an interim deputy. What are your duties, exactly?"

"Whatever's needed. Especially since we have—we *had*—a prisoner to look after."

"I assume you don't mean me."

"I mean the guy Jack locked up the other day. Lou Quentin."

"Jack?"

"Sheriff Ward."

"You said you 'had' a prisoner. Did he get away?"

She shook her head. "You'll have to ask the sheriff about that."

"And was this prisoner one of the two men who tried to the rob the same bank, last week?"

Her eyes narrowed. "How do you know about that?"

"I been in town a few days," Carson said. "I heard one fella got caught but the other didn't. Heard they was wearing masks, and hats pulled low over their eyes."

"You heard right. Nobody knows what the second robber looked like."

Carson mulled that over for a moment. "I think I do."

"What do you mean?"

"I think he might be the same guy who talked me into doing what I did today."

A silence passed. Watching him, she said, "The sheriff told me you were alone, today at the bank."

"Up front, I was. Barnes told me he was going in the back way. Said he knew where most of the money's kept, and that since the attempt last week nobody'd be expecting another try."

"Well then, he wasn't very smart. Since last week they've had guards posted in the back, just outside the vault. Around the clock."

"I didn't say he was smart. But he was sure smarter than I was, for listening to him."

"Barnes, you said?"

"That's the name he used. I imagine he's long gone by now."

"I expect so." She scratched her chin—an extremely attractive chin, he thought—and said, "What name do *you* use?"

"Carson. I'm Dave Carson."

Both of them fell silent. Carson sat there in his socks on the edge of the bed, feeling sorry for himself. His gun-belt was still strapped on, minus the gun, but his hat was missing and the rope around his wrists had been tied by somebody who knew what knots to use.

After a long pause he focused again on his jailer. "Where you from, Deputy?"

"Right here in Shady Glen. All my life."

"What do you do, when you ain't deputying?"

"I'm a part-time schoolteacher."

"You joshing me?"

"Want me to recite the multiplication tables?" She paused. "And why are you smiling?"

"Shady Glen. It's a strange name."

"It's a stupid name. As I understand it, a glen's sort of a narrow valley. The land here's flat as a pancake. And the only shade to be found is under a roof, or"—she touched the brim of her hat—"the kind you carry around with you, on your head."

Carson shrugged. "Supposed to sound poetic, I guess."

"Probably." She was wearing boots and long pants, like a man. She stretched her legs and crossed them at the ankles. "What about you?"

"What about me?"

"Where are you from?"

"Tennessee."

"Where you headed?" she asked.

"I *was* going to California. Got a friend in San Francisco."

"Girlfriend?"

Carson broke out another grin. "I think you sound jealous."

She gave him another almost-smile. "That's probably because of your head injury. What kind of friend?"

"An old partner. Owes me money, wants me to go into business with him."

"What kind of business?"

He hesitated. "You'll think it's funny."

"No, I won't."

"Banking. My friend owns a bank. And I'm good with figures."

"You're right," she said. "That *is* funny."

"You won't feel that way, when I do it. California's a booming place, these days."

"I've never been there."

"Want to go?"

This time she did smile, a big grin that crinkled her eyes and lit up her face.

"That might be tempting," she said, actually looking tempted, "if we'd met under different circumstances."

He shrugged. "Maybe it's Fate that we met at all."

Deputy Morton seemed to be trying to think of a reply to that when the door behind her rattled, and the moment passed. She blinked, stood, and moved her chair out of the way.

Sheriff Ward, when he stepped into the room, looked like the drawings of tough, square-jawed lawmen Dave Carson had seen on the covers of dime novels. The sheriff glanced at Carson, sizing him up, then at Morton. "Give us a minute, Lena?"

She walked around him, rifle in hand, and disappeared through the doorway. Carson heard her clomp down the wooden steps outside.

"Let me guess," he said to the sheriff. "You're wondering if I'm the bank robber from the other day. Quentin's partner, the one who got away."

"No. I know you're not. Nobody saw his face, but everybody says he was short. You're too tall."

"So what do you need from me?"

The sheriff pushed the door shut. "I need to ask you some questions."

"I have one for you, too."

"I get to go first," he said. "I want to know if you were acting alone, today."

"Why should I tell you that?"

"Because I don't think you were. When I came into the bank, you was just standing there holding a gun on the tellers. Not doing anything, just standing there." Sheriff Ward moved over to the chair, angled it the way he wanted it, and sat. "Like you was waiting for somebody else to do something. Maybe in the back of the bank."

Carson sighed. "That's exactly what I was doing. I already told your deputy that." Then he said, "My question is, why were *you* there?"

"Because I was summoned."

"What?"

"A guy stormed into the jail, where my office is, and said come quick—the bank's being robbed."

Carson blinked. "He said what?"

"You heard me."

"But nobody else *knew* it was being robbed."

"Somebody did. And this fellow was real short."

Dave Carson's shoulders sagged. *Barnes*, he thought. It had to be him. And it wasn't hard to believe that he'd also been in on the robbery a week ago.

What *was* hard to believe was that Carson had gotten involved with him at all. It had seemed a blessing, at the time. Carson's money—every penny he'd owned—had been stolen on the trail two weeks ago, and Emmett Barnes had been the first person he'd met when he rode into Shady Glen. After buying Carson a beer in the saloon Barnes had looked around carefully, leaned forward, and whispered that he knew how to make ten thousand dollars in ten minutes' time, if Carson was interested. When Carson found out it was a bank heist he was understandably skeptical, but Barnes insisted nobody would be hurt and said he had a hiding place ready and waiting for them, half a dozen miles away. Tired and broke and out of options, Carson had—against his better judgment—agreed. And look where it had gotten him, he thought.

"The thing is," the sheriff continued, "nothing got stolen, today, far as I know, and nobody got hurt. Last week neither, but ever since then, there's been a bank guard posted in the back, out of sight beside the vault, and I figure that guard must've stayed put today—like he'd been told to do."

"Wouldn't it be simpler," Carson said, "just to keep the vault locked?"

"Apparently they can't. Tellers are in and out of it all day."

That sounded to Dave Carson like a dumb rule, not that he cared a whit how they ran the bank. What he did care about was what had happened to him, today.

"This man who fetched you," he said. "He set me up. Why'd he do it?"

"I been considering that," the sheriff replied. "I think you were a diversion."

"A what?"

"A diversion, distraction, call it what you like."

That made sense, Carson thought. He remembered standing there scared to death in the bank lobby, holding his revolver on the two tellers and the bank manager, waiting on Emmett Barnes to finish whatever he was presumably doing in the back of the building, when Carson had heard the click of the latch on the front door, behind him. He had whirled around and found himself staring into the barrel of the sheriff's gun. The two stood looking at each other for what seemed a long time, then Carson gave up and lowered his pistol.

"Drop it on the floor," the sheriff said.

When that had been done he walked toward Carson and was picking it up when a thunderous explosion shook the building. Everyone, including Dave Carson, turned to look out the windows. Across the street they saw a towering, boiling cloud of smoke.

"Ain't that the jail?" one of the tellers said.

The sheriff didn't answer. He just shoved Carson's pistol into the hand of the bug-eyed bank manager and said, "This man's under arrest. Watch him."

Then he rushed out the door toward the scene of the blast. Seconds later the manager must've whacked Carson on the head with the gun, as Deputy Morton had said, because Carson blacked out. Why the manager had done it was anyone's guess—maybe he was angry, maybe he was worried about the responsibility of guarding a prisoner, maybe he was just spooked. Whatever the case, that was the last thing Carson remembered.

But he knew the sheriff was right: Carson's role in the bank holdup *had* been a diversion. The man who'd entered the jail and reported a robbery in progress was almost certainly Emmett Barnes. After the sheriff had left, Barnes must've run around back and blown up the jail—

"To kill the man who'd been captured," Carson said. "His former partner. That's it, ain't it? You were holding the other robber—Quentin—in one of the cells."

"Bits and pieces of him are still there," the sheriff said. "And yes, I think you, and this staged robbery today, was part of a plan to get me out and away while this short fella lit the fuse of a charge he must've planted earlier, outside the window of Quentin's cell. Deputy Morton was down at the post office at the time." He tipped his hat back and rubbed his forehead. "We'd been pressuring Quentin to tell us who the other robber was, but he'd refused to talk. I guess this was to make sure he never would."

"But what about me?" Carson said. "The short guy you saw must've known *I* would talk, that *I* would tell you who he is. In fact, I'll tell you right now: his name's Emmett Barnes, from up north someplace—or so he said. But what good would it do him to kill one partner to keep him quiet if he wasn't gonna kill the other, too?"

"I think he tried to," the sheriff said.

"What?"

"I think he wanted *me* to kill you. Understand this: He didn't *just* tell me the bank was being robbed—he said it was being robbed by only one man, a crazy drifter named Dave Carson who'd murdered five ranch hands in south Texas. Said I better shoot this killer quick, before he shot me or somebody else."

Carson took a moment to absorb this news. Then: "So why didn't you?"

"What?"

"Why didn't you shoot me? You had the jump on me—I heard the click of the doorlatch when you came in, while I was still looking the other way, but I was too slow. You could've pulled the trigger then, or even after I turned around to face you—but you didn't."

"Yes, I did," Sheriff Ward said.

In the silence that followed, he took a long, shiny cartridge from his shirt pocket and handed it to Carson. An unfired cartridge; the gray slug was still intact. When Carson looked at the other end of the shell, he saw a tiny indention in its flat center ring.

"I did pull the trigger," the sheriff repeated. "And nothing happened. That click you say you heard? It wasn't the door—I came in quiet. It was the firing pin of my pistol, striking that shell. First misfire I've seen in years." He leaned back in the chair. "That's how close you came to dying today."

"And how close Barnes's plan came to shutting me up, too. Right?"

"Sounds like it to me."

At that instant someone rapped on the door. Sheriff Ward stood and opened it with one hand on his holstered revolver. It was Jasper Luckett, the bank manager. His eyes were wide, his glasses askew, his face beet-red.

"Bad news, Sheriff." he said, panting. "It's the money."

"What money?"

"The cash, in the bank vault."

"What about it?"

"It's gone."

For a full five seconds, the only sound was the rasping of the manager's breath. Then the sheriff said, "What about your guard? You said one of three men's been posted outside the vault, day and night, since last week's robbery attempt."

The manager swallowed hard. "The guard for this shift has been out front in the lobby ever since you left, like everybody else, looking out the window at the burning jail. He left his post because he thought"—he cleared his throat—"we all thought the excitement at the bank was over."

"So, meanwhile, somebody jimmied the back door, strolled through it and into the vault and out again, without anybody even knowing about it?"

"Must have, yeah." Luckett was still puffing like a draft horse.

The sheriff took off his hat and ran a hand through his hair. "Go on back, Jasper. I'll be there shortly. I got something I need to finish, here."

Luckett seemed to notice Carson for the first time and flushed even redder. "You," he growled. "After the sheriff left I shoulda shot you, instead of busting you in the head."

"Why'd you hit him at all?" the sheriff asked.

"'Cause I was mad, that's why."

Behind the sheriff, Carson sighed. "Can't say I blame you for that," he murmured.

"Then your lady deputy showed up, Sheriff, and told us about the damage to the jail, and told us you said to carry him here instead."

"I did. And I bet the vault guard was one of those you asked to help lug Carson over here, right? While your money was being stolen in the other room?"

The miserable look on Jasper Luckett's face confirmed that.

"Get out of here, Jasper." When the bank manager had slunk away, and Sheriff Ward turned to face Carson, the lawman huffed out a sigh.

"What a damn mess," he said.

Carson chose to keep silent.

"Seems our Mr. Barnes was a busy man today," the sheriff said. "We've already established that your little go-round at the bank was nothing but a warm-up, and what I'm thinking now is, even the dynamite at the jail wasn't the main event. It killed Lou Quentin, yes, and that was a plus for Barnes, but in the end, it was just another diversion. Once everybody's attention was on the bonfire across the street and away from your bungled robbery and your capture, Barnes must've circled around behind the bank and got what he really wanted all along."

Carson shook his head. "If all that's true, why didn't he just blow up his partner's cell and then cross the street and loot the bank? Why'd he involve me at all?"

"Didn't you hear what I said to Luckett? They'd assigned a full-time guard at the vault. That guard wouldn't have left his post because the jail blew up. He left it because there'd just been another robbery attempt today, and it failed, and *then* the jail blew up. He thought—everybody thought—the party was over, and the vault was safe."

The little room had gone dead quiet. From somewhere outside, Carson heard the rumble of a passing wagon, and the yapping of a dog. He raised his bound hands again to touch the side of his head. It was still throbbing.

"So what now?" he asked.

"Now I have to catch him. The 'how' is another matter."

"I think I know how," Carson said. He looked up at the sheriff. "I think I know where he went."

The sheriff frowned. "Don't give me that. Don't try to bargain with me. I believe most of what you've told me, Carson, but you can't make me believe this Barnes character told you where he was going with the money. I think he tried to have me kill you, yes, but there was no guarantee that'd work. You could've killed me instead, or I could've just wounded you, or ten other things could've happened. He wouldn't've told you—that'd be too big a risk."

"I didn't say he told me anything. I just said I think I know where he's holed up."

"How could you know that?"

"Because I been here a while," Carson said, "in and out of town. In all that time, the ground's been dry and hard and brown. Everywhere. Maybe yellowish and even greenish a time or two, but never red."

"What are you talking about?"

"I met with Emmett Barnes three different times, and each time he had red dirt on his boots. Fresh red dirt. I ain't from here, but you are. Where would you find dirt like that?"

Sheriff Ward's frown deepened. He gazed out the window for a minute, thinking.

"Reno Wells," he said. "Six miles west of here."

"That the only place?"

"Only one I know about. There's a couple old cabins there."

"Then that's probably where he is."

"You sound pretty certain."

"Barnes mentioned that distance. Half a dozen miles."

The sheriff stayed quiet for a long time, watching Carson's face. Finally, he stood up and opened the door. "I'm sending Deputy Morton back in here. You stay put. If I manage to catch Barnes at the Wells and if I get back here alive..."

Ward fell silent. He seemed to be making up his mind about something.

"If I do that," he said finally, "you're free to go."

Carson blinked. "Are you serious?"

"I am."

"Why? I robbed a bank today."

"You tried to rob a bank. And you seem to be trying hard to help me catch the man who really did. And who blew up half of my jail, and all of my prisoner."

Carson shook his head. "It's something more than that. Why are you doing this?"

After a long pause the sheriff said, "I told you I tried to shoot you, earlier. That was true. I tried to kill you, for what I thought was good reason, and Fate kept me from doing it. It was a miracle, far's I'm concerned—I ain't chambered a dud bullet in ten years. But the thing is, *you* could've killed *me*, too. We stood there ten seconds or more, you and me, guns pointed at each other after I misfired. And you didn't shoot. Why not?"

Carson heaved a sigh. "I never intended to shoot you, Sheriff, or anyone else. I never shot anybody in my whole life. And, for what it's worth, I never been to south Texas, neither."

"I figured not."

The sheriff pulled open the door, paused, and beckoned to someone in the distance. Past him, Carson could see a rail fence, a struggling garden plot, and a stack of what looked like firewood. Yellow dust swirled in the wind.

"What if you don't come back?" he asked.

Sheriff Ward looked at him. "That's a good question."

He put his hat on, creased the sides, and turned to leave.

"One more thing," Carson said.

The sheriff stopped and faced him.

"A while ago you called your deputy 'Lena.' That's her first name?"

"Yep."

Carson nodded, thinking. "She told me she's never seen California."

"No, I expect not." Ward tilted his head, looking thoughtful. "That's where you're going, from here?"

"Soon as you get back."

"I hope you don't plan to rob any banks there."

"I hope you don't get shot."

That got a flicker of a grin. "See you in a couple hours."

Their gazes held for a moment, then the sheriff stepped out and down the steps into the sun. Seconds later Lena Morton appeared in the doorway, rifle in the crook of her arm.

Carson sat there on the bed with his hands bound and his elbows propped on his knees, watching her. Her hat was off, pushed back and held by a thin cord around her neck. Her copper-colored hair stirred in the warm breeze.

"What are you smiling about now?" she asked him.

"Fate," he said.

John M. Floyd's work has appeared in more than 250 different publications, including *Alfred Hitchcock's Mystery Magazine*, *Ellery Queen's Mystery Magazine*, *The Strand Magazine*, *The Saturday Evening Post*, *Mississippi Noir*, and *The Best American Mystery Stories*. A former Air Force captain and IBM systems engineer, John is also a three-time Derringer Award winner and an Edgar nominee. His sixth book, *Dreamland*, was released in 2016.

THE LIST
Charlie Drees

The phone rang, pulling me from the crossword puzzle. "Security, Hunt speaking."

"Be in my office in five minutes."

That was it. No "Hello" or "How are you?" But then, Thomas Daggett, founder and CEO of Daggett Enterprises, wasn't known for making small talk.

"Yes sir," I said, but I was talking to the dial tone.

I cradled the handset and headed to the restroom. Splashing cold water on my face didn't help: the guy staring back at me in the mirror was still middle-aged with gray hair, a paunch, and tired eyes that had seen too much. I cinched my tie. A dried scrap of last night's burrito clung to its tip. I scratched it off, then took a deep breath and buttoned my blazer.

Edwin Hunt reporting for duty.

The elevator rocketed me to the thirtieth floor. The only other time I'd breathed the air up here was when Frank Mitchell, the head of security, showed me around the day I was hired. Soft light glowed from recessed ceiling-fixtures and plush carpeting provided plenty of cushioning for my tired feet. Even the fake Christmas tree in the corner oozed class.

A regal-looking blonde sat behind the receptionist's desk. "May I help you?"

"Edwin Hunt to see Mr. Daggett."

"Go right in; he's expecting you."

Daggett was on the phone, so I cooled my heels. His office was larger than my studio apartment. Plus, it had a killer view. From up here, he could admire the scenery without having to mingle with the riff-raff. The rest of his office was about what I expected: a leather couch and chairs grouped to the side for conversation; a built-in bookcase; sedate prints on the walls.

Daggett hung up and pointed to one of the chairs in front of his desk. "Sit down."

I sank into the soft leather and waited while he eyeballed me. He was a good-looking guy, not that I swung that way. I'd read he was pushing sixty—like me—but he looked a decade younger. He still had his hair although there was some silver threaded through the black. What wrinkles he had suggested character, not aging, and his tan hadn't come from a bottle. His clothes looked expensive. Hell, his monogrammed, white shirt probably cost more than my blazer. A photo on his bookcase showed him behind the helm of a decent-sized sailboat. An attractive woman who looked half his age hovered at his side. Wife or daughter, I couldn't say. But the look on her face suggested awe. He probably got that a lot.

Daggett perched on the edge of his desk. "I have a situation. With Frank out on vacation, I'm stuck with you. He swears you're good. I hope he's right."

I'd heard worse. "You can count on me, Mr. Daggett. I was a good cop for over thirty years."

"Really?" Daggett said. "Internal Affairs said you were dirty. Frank convinced me we could use a man with your... *ability* to get things done. That's the only reason I hired you."

My chest tightened. By now I knew I couldn't escape my past. IA claimed I was "morally flexible" when it came to the law. Me? I'd always thought that Justice was blind for a reason. The straw that broke the camel's back had been a case involving a pedophile. But if I had it to do over again, I'd plant the evidence just the same.

"What can I do for you?"

Daggett handed me a cream-colored envelope. "This came in the morning mail."

The envelope was blank except for Daggett's printed name. From its weight, I expected to find several pages inside, but it contained only one. Same color; same texture; same heft. The paper felt as crisp as a newly starched shirt. I scanned the brief message.

> I've checked my list. You've been very naughty.
> Imagine what people would say if they knew.
>
> Santa.

Daggett's jaw muscles flexed. "I thought it was a joke. But the second line reads like a threat. I don't like threats."

"You have a lot of enemies, Mr. Daggett?"

Daggett paced on the plush carpet. "Of course I have enemies. You don't create a company like mine without making enemies." He turned and faced me. "People in my position may wear white shirts but we get our hands dirty."

I held up the letter. "But you don't want to dirty your hands with this."

Daggett nodded. "Find out who sent it."

Easier said than done. The letter-writer had used a computer printer to type the message. No help unless I found the printer. But the paper was a different story. It was too expensive for a box store or discount joint. If I found out who sold it, I might get a buyer's name. In these digital days, I doubted there were that many people still willing to fork over big bucks for stationery. Trouble was, whoever sent it could have purchased it on-line. Time to start impressing my boss.

"I know a guy who works in the police crime lab. If he can identify who manufactures this paper, I can find out if anyone around here sells it."

Daggett shook his head. "No police. Word could get out, and I can't afford that. I want you to handle this discreetly."

"With all due respect, sir, you're asking me to find a needle in a haystack. Unless I have something to go on, it's practically impossible."

Daggett scowled. "What part of 'no police' don't you understand?"

My face burned. So much for good impressions. "Okay, how about this? You keep the letter, and I'll show my guy the envelope. It'll give me a place to start."

Daggett stared out the window for a moment and then nodded. As I handed him the note, the door opened, and the woman in the sailboat photo stepped inside. She wore her dark hair shorter now, framed against her face. She looked even better in person. Her flawless skin and piercing blue eyes belonged in a fashion magazine. Her gaze swung from Daggett to me.

"Oh, I'm sorry. I didn't know you were in a meeting."

Daggett shoved the letter into a desk drawer. "You could've checked with my secretary."

The woman brushed a wayward strand of hair off her cheek. "She wasn't at her desk."

"What do you want, Eleanor?"

She glanced at me. "Aren't you going to introduce me, Thomas?"

Daggett sighed. "Edwin Hunt, my wife, Eleanor. Mr. Hunt works in Security."

One mystery solved. I tucked the envelope inside my jacket. "We met at the Labor Day picnic."

She tilted her head. "Really? I don't remember."

"What a surprise," Daggett said. "You didn't remember much about that day."

She winced as if she'd been slapped. I waded in before Daggett could scold her again. "I expect you met a lot of people that day, Mrs. Daggett."

Her eyes widened like those of a child who'd received an unexpected gift. "Yes, I did."

Daggett frowned. "Why are you here, Eleanor?"

"I needed to do some Christmas shopping and wanted to see if you'd come along."

"Don't be silly. I'm busy."

Her eyes flashed; a touch of backbone. "You're always busy."

"That's why you can afford to shop," Daggett said. He gripped his wife's elbow and steered her toward me. "Escort Eleanor downstairs and find someone to take her shopping." As I opened the door, Daggett added, "Be sure and take care of that special project."

"Don't worry. I'll get it cleared up in no time."

"See that you do, Mr. Hunt. See that you do."

As we waited for the elevator, Eleanor Daggett smiled at me. "You were quite nice in Thomas' office."

I shrugged. "No big deal."

Her eyes glistened. "It was a very big deal to me." She opened her clutch purse and pulled out an embroidered handkerchief. "I don't get much of that anymore." She dabbed her eyes without smearing her mascara. "Would *you* drive me?"

I smoothed the front of my tie. "Mrs. Daggett, I don't think—"

"I won't take no for an answer. Please?"

What could I say? She was the boss's wife. Maybe *she* knew of a ritzy stationery store and I could kill two birds with one stone. Plus, Eleanor Daggett was pretty easy on the eyes.

"Okay, but we have to keep this between the two of us."

She tugged an imaginary zipper across her lips. "I promise, but only if you call me Eleanor."

I nodded. "Call me Ed."

She linked her arm through mine. "Okay, Ed, let's go shop."

We stormed through department stores the way the Nazis blitzed through France. Three hours later, the trunk was full. We stopped for a late lunch at a posh restaurant where the *maître d'* fawned over Eleanor. He led us to our booth and took her coat. Underneath, she wore a gray tunic-dress with three-quarter length sleeves, cinched at the waist. Classy.

We'd barely settled in our seats when a waiter brought a bottle of wine. She glanced at it, nodded to the waiter, then looked at me. "I hate to drink alone."

"I'm on duty."

She zipped her lip.

I smiled at the waiter. "Pour me what the lady's having."

Eleanor had a good appetite. I had a filet; she had lamb. The waiter kept refilling her glass with wine, but since I was driving, I stopped at one. The wine loosened her lips. As she talked about her marriage to Daggett, there was no awe in her eyes. Just sadness.

Over dessert, she raised her glass for a toast. Her sleeve slid to her elbow revealing an ugly bruise. She slipped her arm under the table and stared at her plate. "I fell in the shower."

I waited until she looked at me. "You'll have to be more careful."

"He's not a monster," she murmured.

I kept my mouth shut. No point in telling her there were shelters for women like her—or that she could divorce him and start over. She had her own reasons for staying.

Afterward, I drove her home to a gated community in the suburbs. The house sat on several acres of wooded ground overlooking a golf course. It looked nice—as far as mansions go—but I figured it was a dusting nightmare.

It took me two trips to unload the trunk. After finishing, I waited in the foyer. Eleanor appeared from one of the back rooms. "I enjoyed that," she said. "You're good company."

I smiled. "My pleasure."

We looked at each other, an edgy silence filling the space between us. Eleanor rubbed her arms. "About what I said at lunch?"

I zipped my lips. She smiled her thanks. I grabbed the door knob, then paused. "By any chance do you know where a guy could buy some really expensive stationery? I'm talking top of the line."

"For your wife?"

"I'm not married. It's not for me."

"Let me think," she said, stroking the base of her throat. "I've heard that Tabula Rasa carries exquisite paper. You might try there."

"You know the address?"

"I believe it's on the corner of Ashmore and Stratton."

"Thanks, I'll check it out."

Eleanor held out her hand. "I had a wonderful time."

"Me, too."

She stood on the porch, watching as I drove away. I made it back to the city and headed for Tabula Rasa. On the way, I had a better idea and detoured to work. Daggett had said the letter arrived in the morning mail. There hadn't been any postage on it, so someone had to give it to the receptionist at the lobby desk or drop it off at the mail room in the basement. All I had to do was find out which.

Of course, it was possible the person behind this could have gotten someone off the street to deliver it. But if Daggett was right about having enemies, I suspected the letter writer would get more satisfaction doing it himself.

Daggett Enterprises had spared no expense when it came to security. Surveillance cameras placed throughout the building captured most everything that went on. My boss, Frank, had told me about servers, network cameras, video streams, but all that went over my head. The part I understood was that all the pictures from each camera were archived in the mainframe, and with a few clicks of the mouse, I could pull up any image I wanted.

I logged on to my computer and clicked on the security icon. I narrowed the search parameters to yesterday between four-thirty and six-thirty. The lobby in our building was open and airy—no pillars to obstruct the view. Even so with all the people bustling about around closing time, a person could slip in and out virtually unnoticed.

I played the feed from the camera in the lobby and spotted my quarry the third time through. The oversized sunglasses gave her away. This time of year, the sun set early; no need for sunglasses. I watched her thread her way through the crowd. In addition to the glasses, the upturned collar on her winter coat partially hid her face. She had on a woolen hat, and her long hair cascaded over her shoulders. She bypassed the elevators and took the stairs.

I switched to the camera covering the mail room and plugged in the time. The computer whirred, and I saw the mystery woman exit the stairwell and head toward the mail window. The clerk ignored her as he pulled down the metal shutter closing the counter space. She pulled an envelope from her pocket and shoved it in the wall slot without breaking stride. Then, she spun around and disappeared back into the stairwell.

I switched back to the lobby camera and let it run. The woman emerged from the stairwell and blended in with the crowd. She marched across the polished terrazzo floor, pushed open the glass door, and disappeared from view. According to the digital timer, the whole episode had taken less than four minutes.

I spent the next twenty minutes re-running the video. Each time I watched, I felt more certain I'd solved the mystery. My hunch wouldn't hold up in court, but Thomas Daggett was the only jury I had to convince.

I printed a few of the better frames and exited the program. I checked my watch: 7:22. I'd worked long past closing time, but I hadn't felt this jazzed since leaving the police force. A smile creased my face. Then a thought popped into my head, and my smile vanished. Had the mystery woman dropped off another letter while I was out with Eleanor? I pulled up the images from the past few hours, but after another hour of searching, I didn't spot her.

My eyes burned, so I called it a night. I logged off my computer, locked the prints in my desk drawer, and turned off the lights. All in all, I'd done a damn fine job of detective work. It called for a celebration. I stopped at the nearest bar and toasted my skills. While I was there, I thought of Eleanor Daggett and the sad look on her face as I drove away.

I toasted her as well.

* * * *

I made it to work before the sun rose. I wanted a front row seat in case the mystery woman made an early-morning appearance. I camped behind the visitor's desk which gave me a clear view of the elevators and the stairwell. The receptionist tried to make small talk, but I didn't feel like chatting. After a while, she gave up.

By 7:15, people began filtering into the lobby. The mystery woman didn't show until the rush hit at 7:50. The digital images had been black and white, so I hadn't known her hair was a deep-red—almost mahogany—color. Today, she wore jogger's tights and a fleece jacket; no hat. I tracked her red hair in the crowd. Once again, sunglasses hid her eyes.

She followed her previous M.O. and disappeared down the stairwell. I grabbed my topcoat and waited by the front door, pretending to read the directory. When she returned, she passed by me, close enough to touch. After exiting the building, she headed north. I waited ten seconds, then followed. The wind had a bite to it. I buttoned my coat and wished I'd brought a hat.

Her red hair made her easy to tail. I dropped back in case she looked over her shoulder, but she never did. We stayed this way for another ten minutes until she crossed the street on a yellow and I got hung up at the curb. She disappeared into a building patrolled by a doorman who tipped his hat as he held open the door.

None of the workout joints I knew about had a doorman, so this must be home sweet home. The doorman put up a fuss, but two Jacksons later I had her name and apartment number: Caitlin Cole, 904. I needed more. "What's her story?"

The doorman turned mute. I forked over another twenty, and he got chatty. "Some sugar daddy pays for her place. No way she could afford it on her own."

"You know his name?"

He shook his head. "No, but I'll tell you one thing: this guy shows up two, three times a week and always leaves with a smile." I opened the door. "Hey, where're you going?" he said.

"To see what makes him smile."

I rode the elevator up to the ninth floor. When it arrived, I held the door for a petite, gray-haired lady carrying one of those small dogs that look like an overgrown hairy rat. To be fair, he didn't seem too impressed with me, either.

I knocked on 904 and waited. Nothing; I knocked again. After a minute, I heard a chain rattle and the lock pop. The door opened, and there she was. Thick red hair, porcelain skin, dark green eyes. The kind of eyes sunglasses shouldn't hide. A tiny mole near the corner of her mouth marred an otherwise perfect face. She had on a green silk robe, cinched at the waist. It complemented her eyes. She cocked her hip and leaned against the door jamb.

"Yes?"

I tilted my head and frowned. "You're not Susan."

"No kidding."

"Is Susan here?"

"There's no Susan here. You've got the wrong apartment."

"Sorry to bother you."

She yawned. "It's okay. I had to get up anyway."

Her door clicked shut. Strange. Why tell me she had to get up if she'd just come home? It didn't make sense, but I'd ponder it later. Right now, I had more important things on my mind. Evidently, Sugar Daddy had used Caitlin to do his dirty work. Once I uncovered his name, I'd serve him to Daggett on a silver platter. Case closed.

I found the doorman standing outside in the cold. "I need the sugar daddy's name."

"I can't tell you that."

"There's a hundred bucks in it for you."

He shook his head. "No way. If he found out, I'd get fired."

"Okay, how about this? I tell your boss you're spilling secrets about the residents. You get fired anyway, *and* you kiss a hundred bucks good-bye."

He glared at me, but in the end, greed won out. "Wait here. I'll be right back."

While he was inside, it started snowing—light feathery flakes that seemed to take forever to fall, like the powder in a child's snow globe. I pictured Eleanor in that big, empty house, staring out a window at the falling snow.

The doorman returned, interrupting my thoughts. He grabbed my elbow and walked me to the curb like he was taking out the trash. "This is it. No more favors."

I passed him five twenties. "Who is he?"

He looked up and down the street. "I thought he looked familiar. His picture's in today's paper, hobnobbing with the mayor."

I shoved my hands into my coat pockets. "His name?"

"Maybe you've heard of him. Thomas Daggett?"

* * * *

Tonya Royce stuck her head in my doorway. She was in charge of the IT department and had hinted around that she liked me. Why, I didn't know. I hadn't done anything to encourage her. Maybe she had a thing for chubby ex-cops.

"There you are," she said. "Daggett's been looking for you all morning."

This morning's letter. I'd forgotten all about it. I grabbed the photo of Caitlin I'd been studying and eased past Tonya. "Tell him you haven't seen me. I'll be back in an hour."

She shrugged. "Your funeral."

The snow continued to fall making travel on the streets an adventure, but I eventually found Tabula Rasa. It was two blocks west of where Eleanor and I had eaten. Inside, there was a lot of chrome and glass and soft lighting. Holiday music hummed in the background. A young sales clerk wearing pearls approached me. Her nametag read: Paige. Go figure.

I handed her the envelope from Daggett's letter. "Do you sell this?"

Paige studied the envelope, rubbing it between her thumb and index finger. She held it up to the light, then nodded. "Yes, I believe it's our Coventry model."

"You're sure?"

"Oh, yes. Do you see this?" She pointed to some faint markings feathered on the paper and launched into a monologue about watermarks and linen content.

My eyes glazed over. "Just show me."

Paige guided me to a glass counter at the rear of the store. She pulled out a box of stationery and lifted its lid. The papers and envelopes nestled inside were identical to those Daggett had received. Paige beamed.

"It's the finest stationery we carry."

"How much?"

"Three hundred dollars for a box of forty." She didn't bat an eye.

I showed her the picture of Caitlin Cole. "Did this woman buy a box?"

Her eyes narrowed. "Why do you want to know?"

"I wanted to buy her some for Christmas."

Paige's eyes lit up; she probably worked on commission. She studied the print for a few moments. "I'm not positive, but I think she purchased a box last week. My boss waited on her." She gazed at the picture again. "Too bad this isn't in color; then I could be sure."

"Why?"

She caressed her pearls. "The woman who bought it had the most beautiful red hair. I wanted to ask her where she got it styled."

I smiled, slipped the photo inside my jacket, and headed for the door.

"Wait," Paige said. "Aren't you going to buy her a box?"

I tossed a wave over my shoulder. *My* Christmas present had come early.

Back at work, I opened an e-mail from Daggett's receptionist. He wanted to see me ASAP. This time, I was ready. I grabbed all the security pictures of Caitlin Cole and headed upstairs. When his receptionist saw me, she pointed to his door.

"He's really angry."

I winked and stepped inside. Daggett marched across his lush carpet and shoved a letter in my face. It was identical to its predecessor—same expensive texture, same rich cream color.

"You said you'd handle this," he said. "Where the hell have you been?"

"Doing my job."

Daggett sputtered, but I ignored him and read the note.

> You're still on my naughty list.
> And bad boys have to pay.
> Instructions will follow.
>
> Santa.

So that was her game. Daggett must have done something to upset her. Maybe he got a little too rough in bed, or maybe Caitlin figured out he was never going to leave Eleanor. In any case, she'd settled on blackmail. I handed the letter back to him. "I know who sent it."

"Who?"

I pulled the computer stills from my jacket pocket and handed them to Daggett. He tried to hide it, but from the way his eyes widened, I knew he recognized her. He scanned the rest of the pictures, then looked at me.

"Are you sure?"

I nodded. "Her name is Caitlin Cole. She lives about ten blocks north of here in that Art Deco building on Thirty-eighth and Park. Apartment 904."

He pretended this was news to him, but he gazed at the photos and shook his head as though he couldn't believe his eyes. I kept talking.

"I traced the paper to a store on Ashmore and showed her photo around. A sales clerk recognized her, said she'd bought the stationery last week."

Daggett trudged over to his desk. He slumped into his high-backed chair and stared at the prints. After a few moments, he took a deep breath and looked at me. "Good work, Mr. Hunt. You deserve a bonus. Let's discuss it later."

"Thanks, Mr. Daggett. You want me to talk to her?"

"No, I'll take it from here."

"You sure? I've had a lot—"

"I said I'd handle it."

The chill in his voice made the hair on my neck bristle. Daggett swiveled in his chair and looked out the window. The meeting was over.

I spent the next hour at my desk, trying to focus on work. Tonya stopped by to flirt but left when I didn't play along. My mind kept drifting to Daggett. He didn't strike me as a forgive-and-forget kind of guy. I grabbed my topcoat and headed out the door.

I'd burned my bridges with Caitlin's doorman, so I headed toward the alley, looking for a back entrance. As I rounded the corner, Thomas Daggett exited the building from a door marked Deliveries. He carried a plastic garbage bag in his hand. My heart ratcheted up a notch, and I ducked back out of the alley. I counted to three, then peered around the corner and watched Daggett head down the alley in the opposite direction. He stopped long enough to toss the bag into a dumpster before disappearing around the far corner.

I pulled the bag out of the dumpster. Inside was a white, monogrammed, dress shirt, several pieces of jewelry, and a blood-stained white towel. I recognized the crumpled piece of stationery at the bottom of the bag. Alarm bells went off in my head.

I entered Caitlin's building through the delivery entrance, then snuck down a short hallway to the lobby. The doorman huddled inside the glass doors, trying to stay warm. A few moments later, he stepped outside, and

I took the elevator to the ninth floor.

I pounded on Caitlin's door in the faint hope I'd misread the situation. "Caitlin?" No response. I pounded harder. "Caitlin, open up."

I snugged my gloves, then tried the doorknob; it was unlocked. My skin tingled as I eased open the door and stepped past the foyer into the living room. Caitlin's body lay sprawled in front of the fireplace. She still had on the green robe, only now, crimson streaks stained the top half. She wouldn't be sending any more letters.

All at once, Daggett's offer to meet me later popped into my mind. With Caitlin dead, I was the only witness to the blackmail. Staring into her lifeless eyes, I knew I'd never live to see any bonus from Daggett. And with me dead, the odds of him getting away with murder would sky-rocket. The doorman would remember me, and I'd be the perfect fall guy. I couldn't let that happen.

Twenty minutes later, I dumped the garbage bag down the trash chute and took the stairs down to the lobby. I went out the back door, found a pay phone outside a convenience store, and called 911. Said I'd heard a scream coming from 904. After that, I settled in the coffee shop across the street from Caitlin's building and waited for the cops to arrive. I left before they brought out her body, but not before I saw a detective carry out a plastic garbage bag.

* * * *

After his arrest, Daggett claimed I killed Caitlin Cole. Sure enough, the doorman picked me out in a lineup, but the cops crossed me off their suspect list after Tonya Royce provided them with images from the security cameras showing me at work. No one was more surprised than me. I never asked how she faked them, and she never said. We've been dating ever since.

Lucky for me, the police never ID'd the anonymous caller. I doubted they tried all that hard given the evidence they had on Daggett. At the trial, I testified about the letters and Daggett's order to find the blackmailer. His lawyer tried to punch holes in my testimony, but I stuck to my story. In the end, the jury found Daggett guilty of premeditated murder. At a news conference, one of the jurors said the letters had provided the motive, but it was Caitlin's blood on Daggett's monogrammed white shirt that sealed his fate. Last I heard, his lawyer was appealing his death sentence.

I didn't lose any sleep over committing perjury—or planting evidence. I'd seen the bruises on Eleanor's arm, and the calculated way Daggett decided Caitlin had to die. Daggett was a bad man; he deserved what he got. End of story. Maybe IA was right about me after all.

Eleanor divorced Daggett in the spring, after the trial ended. I heard through the grapevine that as part of the divorce settlement she planned to take over as CEO of Daggett Enterprises. All she needed was the Board of Directors' approval. Before that happened, I wanted to talk with her. Call it unfinished business.

I made the call and trekked to the suburbs. We sat in a sun-filled room at the back of the house sipping freshly-squeezed lemonade. I had a nice view of the manicured lawn and the swimming pool. The snow-covered streets of winter were distant memories.

Eleanor sipped some lemonade. "I haven't had any alcohol since Thomas was arrested."

"Good for you, Mrs. Daggett."

"Mrs. Daggett? What happened to Eleanor?"

"You weren't my boss, then."

She smiled at me over the rim of her glass. "I'm not your boss... *yet.*" She crossed her legs. Her blue sundress matched the color of her eyes. "You said we needed to talk."

I sat my glass on the coffee table and cut to the chase. "I know you sent the letters."

Except for a slight flare of her nostrils, she didn't react. "I don't know what you're talking about."

"We both know better," I said. "It always bothered me that Caitlin told me she'd just gotten up that morning. She had no reason to lie to me, so I must have followed someone else. Someone who could masquerade as Caitlin and who knew about your husband's violent streak. Someone who knew how he'd react to blackmail. You with me so far?"

She placed her glass next to mine. "I'm all ears."

"Good. Here's the kicker: I staged the crime scene."

Eleanor perked up. "But you testified—"

"I lied. I got there after your husband killed her. I saw him toss the garbage bag into a dumpster. I dug it out and took it upstairs to her apartment. I smeared her blood on his shirt, then called the cops and told them to check the trash chute."

"Why would you do that?"

"I didn't want him to get away with murder. Simple as that."

She settled back in her chair. "I see. So what makes you think I'm involved?"

"That building has a back door. It's how your husband and I got in and out that day without being seen. It also explains how the mystery woman could've given me the slip."

"I still don't see a connection to me," she said.

"The stationery," I said. "I searched Caitlin's apartment but never found any. The sales clerk at Tabula Rasa said the woman bought a box. A box holds forty sheets and twenty envelopes. There should've been some left."

"You were at the trial," Eleanor said. "The police speculated she wrote letters to other people."

"None of her friends or family ever got one. I checked. They all said she kept in touch through e-mail or Facebook."

Eleanor picked a piece of lint off her dress. "Maybe she was trying something different."

I shrugged. "Maybe, but it got me thinking. What were the odds that you'd send me to the only store in the entire city that sold that brand of stationery?"

"If I sent the letters, why would I tell you where to find the stationery?"

"Because you knew I was looking for the blackmailer," I said. "You knew your husband had received the letter. You saw it when you dropped in on us. He told you I was with Security, and you put two and two together. Then when I asked you about expensive stationery, you steered me toward Tabula Rasa. You knew someone would remember a woman who'd spent three hundred bucks on paper. Especially a woman who looked like Caitlin Cole."

"That's ridiculous," Eleanor said. "I told you about Tabula Rasa because friends of mine shop there, not me. If that… *woman* shopped there, it was a coincidence. Nothing more."

"I was a cop for over thirty years. There's no such thing as coincidence."

"That's it? That's all you've got?"

I shook my head. "No, there was something I didn't notice until the trial. I'm surprised nobody else caught it. Remember when the DA showed the photos of Caitlin—the ones from the security cameras and the one her friend took of her wearing her sunglasses at the beach?"

Eleanor stared into space, then nodded. "Everyone gasped."

"The photos looked like a match. They seemed to prove Caitlin was the mystery woman."

"*Seemed* to prove?"

"That's when I knew you sent the letters."

Eleanor stood up and walked to the door. "I've heard enough."

"The mystery woman didn't have a mole."

She spun around. "What?"

I touched a spot next to my mouth. "Caitlin had a mole right here. The woman in the security photos didn't. And neither do you."

"So what? A lot of women don't have moles."

"But their husbands weren't having affairs," I said. "Their husbands didn't beat them. Their husbands didn't need to be… *punished*. I bet if I searched your house, I'd find green-tinted contact lenses, a red wig, and the stationery."

"You'd lose that bet," she said. "But even if what you say is true—and I'm not saying it is—it's not a crime to play dress up. Or send your husband cryptic notes."

I borrowed a line from the first letter. "Imagine what people would say if they knew."

Her eyes widened. "You're trying to blackmail me."

I climbed to my feet. "I prefer to think of it as balancing the scales."

She looked more amused than angry. "What's your price? Fifty thousand?"

"Don't insult me," I said.

She sneered. "Aren't you the ambitious one? Okay, a hundred thousand." When I didn't answer, her smirk disappeared. "How much?"

I strolled over to the window and admired the view. "That's the trouble with people like you. All that money seduces you, makes you think you're entitled to do whatever you want, even if someone gets destroyed in the process. And if there's a problem, you throw money at it to make it go away." I turned toward her. "I don't want your money."

She crossed her arms. "Then what *do* you want?"

"Tell the board that you decided you don't want to run Daggett Enterprises."

"You must be joking."

"I don't joke about murder."

"And if I don't, what're you going to do?" Eleanor asked. "Tell the police?"

I shook my head. "No, my problem is I've got a theory but no proof. And without any hard evidence, the cops'll never believe me. Not with my history."

"Then why are we even having this conversation?"

"Because your ex-husband *would* believe me. He still has money, and I bet he's made some new friends in prison by now. Friends who'd do anything if the price was right."

The color drained from Eleanor's face. "You wouldn't dare."

"Try me."

"Why are you doing this?"

"I told you: to balance the scales. Your ex-husband's already paying his debt. Sooner or later, he'll get the needle. But you're living the good life even though you set this whole thing in motion. I might not have enough evidence to put you away, but I can hit you where it hurts."

"I could tell Thomas you planted the evidence."

"Be my guest. But since I've got an iron-clad alibi, who do you think he'll believe? And just so you know, if anything funny happens to me, my lawyer will send a letter to him detailing all of this."

"You're contemptible. I can't believe I ever thought you were nice."

"At least I'm not a murderer."

Eleanor stared out the window a long time. Finally, she looked at me. "Fine, I'll tell the board I've changed my mind."

"Smart choice."

"How do I know I can trust you?"

I zipped my lips.

Charlie Drees is an unabashed mystery fan. His stories have appeared in *The Prosecution Rests, By Hook or by Crook: The Best Crime and Mystery Stories of 2009,* and *Girl Trouble.* A member of Mystery Writers of America, Drees is working on a mystery novel set in the Midwest.

SOMETHING CERTAIN
Peter W. J. Hayes

First, she was aware of how wet her face was, how her vision was steeped in red. She wiped her eyes with her hand and streaks appeared in the redness. The taste in her mouth was copper, and she understood the meaning. But her body didn't hurt anywhere, and she was glad for that. Above her a canopy of tree branches interlocked below a wide blue sky and she accepted she was in a forest, on her back, looking up. Slowly, she grew aware of noises, of the shush of tree leaves moving in the wind, the ticking of hot metal as it cooled, and an occasional sizzling sound. Her mind settled, and she recognized a pattern to the sizzles, as if a liquid was dripping slowly onto hot metal. She decided she would try to stand.

And then she was upright. Slowly, she took in her surroundings.

Paper money littered the forest floor. Hundreds, twenties, fifties. The bills shifted sluggishly whenever the breeze strengthened. She pivoted slowly and at a quarter turn saw Freddy on his hands and knees, his white-painted face hanging low between his arms, his orange curly-haired wig somehow still in place. Blood soaked the thigh of his blue polka-dotted costume.

Still the clown, she thought.

He coughed, racked by it, and pawed at the ground with his white kid gloves. She realized he was trying to recover his red foam nose, which lay on the ground a few feet away.

Another quarter turn brought the pick-up into view, or what was left of it. The front of it was wrapped around a tree—a red oak, she noted idly—remembering Mr. Ribar's tenth grade tree project from six years before. Based on the thickness of the trunk she estimated the tree was seventy years old. At the time she couldn't understand why she liked the project. Later, she realized she was attracted to how tree names and their descriptions never changed. They were certain. Something to hold onto as her mother moved her through an endless string of apartments and run-down farmhouses. A pin oak was always a pin oak, a red maple always a red maple, no matter how many boyfriends her mother dragged home.

She took a careful step toward the truck. The bed of the pickup was bent upward in the center like an accordion fold. An arm dangled from the mangle of wreckage where the cab had been. She stepped again, not quickly, drawn to the arm, understanding who she would find. Karl. Karl, with his large hands and sharp brown eyes. The jutting eyebrow ridge that gave him the look of an eagle. His tight jeans. She'd remembered the moment he walked into the bar, his dirty blond hair down to his shoulders, Freddy trailing him with a goofy grin on his face. She took another step. A single line of blood tracked the length of his arm and dripped from a motionless middle finger. What she could see of his body was no farther than two feet from the tree.

She turned and stared at the road embankment. She knew where Karl had lost control. It was the tight corner about a mile west of Ritter's Farm Supply. Anyone from this part of Southwestern Pennsylvania knew the turn and the sudden drop in the road, knew to slow down. She had warned him. But Kurt wasn't from Pennsylvania, and he certainly didn't listen to women.

She gave a final glance at what remained of him, surprised at how little it disturbed her. She'd fallen so hard for him that first night. She'd been aware of his steady eyes watching her as she served him, she'd even liked the touch of arrogance in them. As she pulled their drafts she'd seen how Freddy studied everyone, evaluating them. She guessed they were running from something, guys passing through, but she also knew they were her ticket out, she was sure of it. Because she had to get out. She'd known it when she turned thirteen and suddenly understood the way her mother's boyfriends looked at her body. Later, after pain killers and heroin scythed her high school class, as she and her remaining friends dribbled out of high school to the military or dead-end jobs, she promised herself. She would get away. Demi Moore had grown up down the road in Perryopolis and made it to Hollywood. It was possible, she was certain of it. And somehow, she knew that Karl and Freddy were the ticket.

She heard it then, away in the distance: a siren.

She glanced at the bed of the truck. They weren't supposed to ride there, but things hadn't worked out as expected at the casino. They had improvised when Karl insisted on driving. She understood that as the truck left the road embankment she was thrown clear. She was small and light enough. Freddy, at six feet and more than 200 pounds, with that little sag of stomach that always hung over his belt, he would have needed the impact to be ejected. And then she thought of the bags. All four had been in the bed of the truck with them.

The siren drew closer.

Carefully, still expecting pain to overwhelm her or to be struck by dizziness, she circled the truck. There, scattered on the forest floor, were the bags. Heavy, dirty white canvas things with the logo of the armored truck company on the side. Leather tops and handles. One gaped open at the top, paper money surrounding it and spreading slowly with the breeze. More certain on her feet, she walked among them and hefted each bag, searching for the heaviest.

Karl had explained it to her a few months after he and Freddy moved into the small farmhouse she rented. They were buzzed, a few beers each and a shared joint strong, Freddy out picking up a pizza. Holding a dollar bill in the air Karl asked her, "You know what this weighs?"

"I don't know, half an ounce?" She remembered she was giggling, something she caught herself doing when she was unsure of his line of thinking but wanted to keep his attention.

"A gram. Do you know anything?"

The sharpness of his question sobered her. "I knew that." Her smile was tight as she attuned to his mood. "I knew a guy who dealt coke. He sold it by the gram, bought it by the half pound."

The boys she knew from high school would have immediately asked who the guy was, their questions circling toward exactly how well she knew him. They would have shown some jealousy. Freddy was like that, but Karl just turned down the corners of his mouth as if she wasn't paying attention. "Okay. Every bill made by the government. It weighs a gram. A dollar bill, ten dollar bill, a hundred dollar bill. No difference. One gram."

She had an idea where he was going, then, and relaxed. Also, he liked to explain things to her and she knew it was best to wait. Even if he did take a long time to get to the point.

"So," he said, "if you know every bill's a gram then you know how much a bunch of money weighs. A hundred thousand dollars in hundred-dollar bills is how many grams?"

She waited, acting as if she was having trouble working it out. Karl only asked questions he knew the answers to; he liked how it made him look smart. Freddy asked questions when he didn't know the answer, and she preferred that. She liked how he wanted to understand things.

"One thousand," she said eventually, phrasing it as a question, as if she was unsure of herself. But she'd always been good at math. She loved its precision in the same way as Mr. Ribar's tree project. Every formula led to a precise answer. That brought her a calmness, so different from her father's letters from prison. Those rants about his lawyers, the judge, every other word a curse, made her feel dirty. Mathematics, like the trees, restored her. Both were certain and true. The same way it was true that

Karl liked her better when she was unsure of herself.

Karl leaned toward her. "Right, but how many pounds?"

In her head the answer fell into place, but she picked up her phone, opened the calculator app and ran the computation. "Four," she said, studying the answer on the screen as if it surprised her.

"Exactly." He smiled broadly, his eyes dark, as if she was a prize student. "So, a million dollars in hundreds. What would that weigh?"

She let a frown crease her brow as she worked through the answer in her head, then pecked at the calculator. It produced the same result.

"Twenty-two pounds?" she asked, stressing her uncertainty. But as she spoke she was thinking that Karl was finally going to tell her what he and Freddy were up to. For three weeks they had been slipping out at different times of night and day, returning hours later, their heads close together in conversations that stopped the moment she walked into the room.

"Yeah. You got it!" His smile widened and that was always a problem for her. When he smiled his brown eyes darkened and turned liquid. They undid her every time, despite the way he treated her. She tucked her legs under her on the couch and snuggled against him.

"Can you lift twenty-two pounds?" he asked her.

She settled her head against his shoulder and smelled him, that odd mixture of pine and oil that she could never quite put her finger on. The first time they kissed she thought his smell might be related to his job, but she learned later he and Freddy had lost their fracking jobs three months earlier, so it was only him.

"I think so. How much does a case of beer weigh?" she asked. "I carry them up from the basement to stock the bar all the time."

She felt him stiffen and guessed he didn't know. The door banged, and Freddy walked in, carrying the pizza and a plastic bag of chicken wings that swung like a pendulum. Karl never answered the question, but she had already done the math. Each bottle contained twelve ounces, twenty-four bottles, that was eighteen pounds. Add the weight of the bottles. She figured twenty-two pounds easy.

She kept working the problem in her mind as Freddy placed the food boxes on the table and she removed paper plates from the cupboard.

"Doesn't a fluid ounce weigh more than a weight ounce?" she asked them both, as Freddy opened beers.

"Yeah," said Freddy. Before latching onto the fracking company Freddy had worked on an oil rig near Galveston, and she guessed that measuring fluids was something he understood. He swigged his beer and looked at her. "Fluid is heavier, not by much, I just don't remember how much. Google it." He gave her the lopsided smile that she thought was goofy but liked nevertheless.

She nodded and looked at Karl, who was holding up the pizza box lid and staring at the pie. He always picked out the first slice.

"No problem," she said to him. "Twenty-two pounds is no problem."

Instead of acknowledging her he chose a slice thick with toppings and dropped it on his paper plate.

* * * *

The siren was now close enough that it overwhelmed the birdsong and leaf rustle. A bag in each hand she crossed to Freddy, who had raised himself onto his knees, his head back and eyes as blank as the sky. Absurdly, his red nose was back in place. The bright red lipstick that outlined his mouth was smudged. She bent over and kissed him on the forehead, her lips leaving a perfect imprint on the white greasepaint.

She crossed into the woods then, moving between a pair of red oaks toward a stand of white pine. Behind her the surging high note of the police cruiser's engine dropped sharply. The driver knew the corner and had slowed, she realized, surprised that a statey would be familiar with the road.

Then she was through the pines and into a pipeline cut, the cross-country kind, the trees set back fifteen feet on each side. She moved alongside the pipe, gliding easily now, the bags almost light in her hands. She'd been right about carrying twenty-two pounds, all those nights ago. She remembered that. And she recalled how after the pizza and a few more beers she had gone to the bedroom she shared with Karl, slid out of her clothes and into a t-shirt and gym shorts for bed, only to have Karl stagger into their room and challenge her to carry twenty-two pounds. It was the first time he had spoken to her since she had asked him the weight of a case of beer.

He made her come downstairs to a duffel he'd packed with rocks from the border of the flower garden in the yard. Her bathroom scale was nearby.

"Lift it," he'd ordered.

She did, walking easily back and forth in the living room.

"Okay," he breathed, then grabbed a small knapsack and disappeared outside. A few minutes later he'd created a second weighted bag and told her to carry both. She did, out of the living room and into the kitchen, where Freddy sat at his laptop. Lugging one in each hand meant that her arms were pinned to her sides, and as she walked her breasts bounced under her tight t-shirt.

She saw how Karl watched her chest, how being unable to move her arms made his eyes glitter. He was punishing her, in his own way, for asking him a question he couldn't answer. Freddy was guarded and avoided looking at her, and she understood that Freddy recognized Karl's treatment of her and didn't like it. She hadn't minded, really. She told herself she held a million dollars in each hand, knowing that Karl asked her the questions only because he planned to have her carrying that kind of money sometime soon.

And now, hiking along the pipeline cut, she actually was. Somehow the weight was manageable, and she grew more positive. She stopped sometimes to rest, standing on different hillcrests and staring across wide swathes of western Pennsylvania's green rolling hills, the view marred only by the occasional drilling platform. Behind her all she heard was the rustle of a gentle wind and the occasional birdsong. She was astounded at her energy, although she had come to understand that her hair was matted on one side, clotted by blood, she guessed, but she didn't care. There would be plenty of time to wash it out.

She walked until darkness gathered in the hollows and among the trees. At the crest of the next hill she stopped to rest and placed the bags on the ground. As she searched the horizon she thought that perhaps she knew the statey who had slowed for the corner. David something. Two years ahead of her in high school, she had liked him and caught him staring at her more than once.

But he had never asked her out, which was a pity, because she would have gone. There had been something steady and sure about him. Something certain. She smiled at how funny that would be, for David to find the truck.

She searched the horizon, her eyes drawn to a light. There, perhaps half a mile away in the fading day, was a farm. Parked next to the barn was a pick-up. She felt buoyant. In farm country, she knew, everyone left their keys in the ignition or above the sun visor. It seemed too early for darkness to fall, but even that was lucky. It would be dark when she reached the farm, easier to steal the truck. Then it would be simple. West toward Cleveland over the farm roads. Clean herself up in a rest area. A few more hours and then sleep in a motel somewhere, paid for with cash. She was amazed at how well everything was turning out. How lucky she was.

She had to hand it to Karl and Freddy, their original plan was well thought out, something she hadn't expected when they sat her down to explain it. By then she knew her original guess about them being on the run was correct, that after losing their fracking jobs they headed south from the New York state line, robbing the local banks favored by the fracking companies. She'd guessed it started as revenge for losing their jobs, until they got the hang of it and found they liked it.

Freddy was the one who laid it out, Karl nodding, looking paternal somehow. It was the casino thirty miles down the road. Freddy explained how the cash room was too well guarded. The better option, he explained, was the weekly armored car delivery. For about two minutes the back of the armored truck was open while they stacked cash on a cart and signed paperwork. The exchange took place on the loading dock behind the casino. They showed her video of the delivery and timed it out. They even knew the location of the security cameras and how many casino guards came outside to help with the delivery. She was impressed.

"Casino security is unarmed," Kurt cut in, and she knew he was trying to make the robbery sound simpler than it was.

"The problem is that we need a distraction." She was aware of Freddy watching her as he talked. "The loading dock is in the open. They can see us coming from a mile away and they'll be ready for us. We need to distract them, so we get the drop on them."

"My idea was for you to show up topless," Kurt said, a loose smile on his face. She was surprised at how cold she felt when he said it.

Freddy ignored him. "There's a dumpster for cardboard and recycling on the dock. So I'm thinking I hide in there. They exchange the money and I step out, but I'll be dressed as a clown. They're all looking at me, trying to figure it out, and Kurt comes up from the side of the truck. Gets 'em covered."

She smiled then, understanding his thinking. A clown costume sounded ridiculous, but it would make it harder to ID him on the security camera footage and he could easily hide a weapon in the loose costume. She guessed he had identified the problems first, then come up with the disguise to solve them. She said that.

Freddy relaxed. "Exactly. But, we need you to drive the truck." He placed a Google Maps satellite picture in front of her and pointed to a parking lot at the back of the casino. "This lot overlooks the loading dock. There's no connecting road, but the hill separating them is grass. As soon as Karl has the drop on them you drive down the embankment and pull up beside the armored truck. We throw the bags in the back, hop in and take off." His eyes searched her face. "Can you do that?"

"Sure she can," said Karl. "And if she did it topless it would be even better."

Freddy didn't shift his gaze. He waited to hear what she had to say.

She thought about it for a moment. "And then we are absolutely out of here? Where do we go?"

"West," said Freddy. "Dump the truck in Cleveland, cash for a new car. Take our time. Keep moving. Cash for everything."

"Then I can do that," she answered.

Freddy dropped his gaze, but she saw a flicker of sadness in his eyes. He actually didn't want her involved, she realized, and as quickly understood why. She was sleeping with Karl, but Freddy was in love with her. She was sure of it. He wanted to protect her from danger. But she knew the plan was Freddy's, it was his careful thinking, and she trusted him. She realized how much she liked him then, his thinking, his feelings for her.

"How much do we get?" she asked.

"Millions," said Karl.

Freddy wiped the table with his hand. "Last two deliveries it's been four bags. We went into the casino a couple of times and bought and cashed out chips. They had no problem giving us hundreds. If we're lucky at least one of the bags is all hundreds. Two at the most. The others will be smaller bills. From the way the guards handle the bags they've got to be over twenty pounds each." He raised his eyes to her. "You can do the math." His tone told her he knew about her act with Karl. That he understood how she liked math.

"Millions," said Karl again.

"Even split three ways," said Freddy. "However much it ends up being."

And here she was. Halfway to the farm now, darkness deepening in a way that made her feel part of it. But her shoulders were supple, her feet moved over the ground so easily it was almost as if she was floating. A new kind of elation overtook her. She changed her angle of approach to the truck to stay hidden from the farmhouse. As she drew closer something rose from her chest, a joy so strong that it radiated outward, and she found she couldn't stop smiling.

* * * *

Trooper David Kass recognized the corner and slowed automatically. At sixty his cruiser bottomed as it hit the sudden drop in the road but the beefed-up suspension handled the sway and he spotted fresh skid marks on the grassy berm as he shot by. He slammed on his brakes and reversed. Climbing out he looked over the embankment and saw the wrecked truck, the clown on his knees looking at the sky, the paper money swirling about, all lit by shafts of sunlight angling through the tree canopy.

He radioed in the location and climbed down the embankment. The clown was barely conscious, but he handcuffed him as a precaution, his boots pressing hundred-dollar bills into the ground. He noted a perfectly placed kiss imprinted on the greasepaint of his forehead. He looked up at the road embankment and saw how the truck tires had not hit dirt until they were ten feet from the road, then the slewing scrape of the wheels for another ten feet right into the tree.

He crossed to the driver's side door, saw the dangling arm and how the truck's steering wheel and most of the engine were crushed into the cab. He tightened, his face hardening automatically into the attitude he was teaching himself to use whenever he pulled someone over or had to handle a situation. The attitude wasn't natural to him yet, although he could feel himself becoming more comfortable with it, and now it helped him ignore the turn in his stomach. There was nothing he could do for the man.

He circled the truck and found the bags from the armored truck. He shook his head slowly, staring at the scene, realizing that he would describe it for years to come. The shifting paper bills, the angled sunlight, the man crushed in the cab, the dazed clown with the red nose. The perfect kiss on the clown's forehead.

A moral about how things go wrong.

He crossed to the figure motionless on the ground. A young woman lay on her back, staring sightless at the sky, blood drying on her open eyes. As he squatted next to her recognition dawned. He knew her. She'd been a couple of years behind him in high school; she worked at the bar near town. In high school he'd thought about asking her out but had been too shy.

He saw the rock jutting out of the ground, how her skull was impaled on it. She had no pulse. He carefully closed her eyes, the touch of her staying on his fingertips, along with her blood. As he pulled his hand away he suddenly understood her expression. Her smile. It was a smile of joy, as if everything had gone her way, as if all her troubles were behind her. As if she'd finally got the one thing she truly wanted.

He didn't understand why, but he knew instinctively that he would never tell anyone this part of the story. About her smile. But as he stared at her the attitude he was nurturing hardened even more. He didn't know it then, but over the years that attitude would gradually take over, become simply who he was and how he carried himself. He would never marry. He would find fewer and fewer chances to laugh.

But he would always remember the joy on her face. A smile so perfect it made him anguish over why he never asked her out. In time he came to believe that—whatever she had found—it was matched by something he had lost.

It wasn't a perfect explanation, but it was the one he chose. Over the years he held it close to him. And it was why, every spring, until age made him unable, he would buy flowers and place them on her grave.

✗

Peter W. J. Hayes is a former marketing executive turned mystery and crime writer. His stories have appeared in various anthologies, magazines and on-line publications, including *Malice Domestic #12*, the *Literary Hatchet*, *Mystery Weekly*, *Mysterical-E*, *Shotgun Honey* and *Yellow Mama*.

THE MOMENT OF RIGHTING
Robb T. White

"You look like you been living rough since I last saw you," I said to him.

"Go to hell," Jake said. Then he laughed and gave me one of those Hollywood man-hugs you see on TV when bros meet up after a long absence.

But I wasn't exaggerating. He looked twenty pounds thinner, his face was gaunt, lean as a fox. I remembered the happy-go-lucky pig face of our high-school days. That was before all my trouble with drinking and the divorce with Cindy—or, I should say, Cindy's lawyer who took everything—kids, house, furniture, the family dog and cats—everything but the clothes on my back. One thing after another until my roofing business folded and my face nearly wound up on that Dead-Beat Dad poster at highway rest stops.

"You look great, man," Jake lied.

"Been okay," I lied right back; "doing fine, you know. Just trying to get the business restarted."

You know that snowball in hell people talk about? I had the same chance of getting a business loan as one of those rolling through hell and making it all the way. That loan officer at KeyBank smirked at my application. The night before, I woke up in some bar's parking lot at daybreak, my head stuffed with cotton and my bladder about to explode. After Cindy kicked me out, it got worse: hanging out with desperate lowlifes, cadging drinks, and waking up next to a woman in some bedbug-infested motel off the interstate. When the booze fog lifted, we'd exchange looks that said the same thing: *What am I doing with this loser?*

Jake wanted to go for coffee, talk about old times. Coffee never happened. It was top-shelf bourbon with an occasional water behind it. It was one in the afternoon when I realized I was totally lubricated. Not a new low for me, but close.

Jake had stopped matching me drink for drink at some point so when he made his pitch, it sounded good. Too good to be true, as they also say.

He'd been sailing the Caribbean for the last seven years, he said. His dream since high school was to own a bar in some Caribbean hot spot for tourists. We laughed at him then. Right off, I'd noticed his deep tan and the sun-bleached hair when we met downtown that day. Coming out of the bar into the blinding light of day, I noticed his skin was bronzed right into the creases on his neck with those pale half-moons under his eyes from wearing sunglasses. Jake's eyes were as blue as ever but they cut from side to side too often. He reminded me of *SafariLive* on *YouTube* when some animal approaches a watering hole wary of predators sneaking up on it.

I'd blurted out too much about my recent run of bad luck. He told me he'd had his share of it, too, like how Hurricane Irma had damaged his fishing boat or a partner had screwed him out of money he was saving for his tropical island bar. On and on, but I wasn't too drunk to recall that Jake was a degenerate gambler even as far back as high school. I figured he'd lost it at the Vegas card tables or on internet gambling. His own family cut him off years ago because he'd embezzled cash from the furniture store his parents owned.

Jake proposed we both take some time off, let Lady Luck find some other guys to mess about. He knew a wealthy couple from New Zealand looking for two deckhands for a Caribbean cruise on their sailboat. They were heading for the Windward Islands at summer's end.

"I know Jack-shit about sailboats," I exclaimed. I was still too drunk to see how bizarre the idea was.

"You sailed ore boats years ago right out of high school," he said.

I laughed. "Those were Great Lakes freighters, man. Floating factories. Painting and scraping all day, handling cables in port. I was an ordinary seaman, a lousy deckhand. I can't tie a bowline to save my life."

"Forget that shit," he said. "We've got a week before we meet the *Cassie* in the Outer Banks where she's being refitted. I can teach you everything you need to know by then."

Jake was vague about where he was staying in town, but I figured he'd had a reconciliation with his parents. Neither of us had vehicles, it turned out. Jake told me he kept his Jaguar and SUV in storage while he worked the yachts and cabin cruisers for the idle rich. We shook hands and I agreed to meet him at the bus depot in the morning.

* * * *

The *Cassie* turned out to be a sleek Bucket racer, one-hundred-twenty feet from beam to stern, plush, white cabin interior, stainless-steel kitchen and a pair of staterooms. It slept eight, although the quarters for two deckhands below the fantail were barely wide enough for one to pass the other. Her real name in Gothic lettering across the stern was *Cassiopeia,* a goddess whose vanity nearly caused her daughter to be eaten by a sea monster sent by Poseidon.

"She's a beauty," Jake said. "But nothing like that Hatteras of mine."

I'd heard so much about his Hatteras 100 on the way down in a sweltering Greyhound bus I wanted to call him out as a bullshitter right there under the bright Carolina skies with the pungent stink of diesel and rotting fish bobbing near the pilings. I'd heard enough about its massive flying bridge, the touch-screen technology, how big the staterooms were and how fast its twin diesels powered it through the turquoise waters of one Caribbean island after another. I never doubted he'd sailed for some rich guy with a Hatteras, but I doubted he ever owned one. It was a pipe dream, like his bar on the beach with tiki torches and palm fronds and the dozens of luscious college women who'd flock to it every night.

"Let's go back to the motel," I said. "I need a cold one."

"No alcohol, Pete. We agreed. I've got five days to make you a saltwater sailor."

Jake took the ruse seriously. He had me studying printouts from the public library on sailing that covered everything from maintenance to emergency procedures. I studied until I was bored stupid. He also grilled me on the facts of my "legend," all fake except for my passport and driver's license.

"This guy, Nusbaum," I complained, "he'll never buy this horseshit about my experiences on world cruises."

"He's a retired surgeon with a heart condition," Jake replied. "He knows sailing vessels like you know how to flog the bishop. He'll be tough to fool. Pete, man, you got to believe it yourself!"

His voice rose with passion and something else—a desperation, as if everything depended on my getting a berth on the *Cassie*.

Jake had met the couple online, some bulletin board catering to wealthy yachtsmen. Being a schmoozer, he convinced this Nusbaum to hire him sight unseen and even got him to hold off on a second hire until he and the wife had a chance to meet me.

"Time to hit the books again," Jake said.

I spent the next three hours answering questions about tidal currents, reefs, and landmarks any Caribbean sailor should know and boned up on my fake past. Jake had me rub the palms of my hands over a cement block he'd picked up from a nearby construction site. I needed rough sailor's hands, he said, for the moment I would be shaking hands with the doctor. He coached me on knot-tying and demanded I sit on a chair in the motel's parking lot, baking in the sun to darken my skin.

"You're pale as a ghost," he'd observed with a sailor's scorn for the landlubber.

My enforced sobriety made me recognize this was no game for Jake; it was cramming for a Big Test. Nothing seemed left of the easy-going guy I'd once hung out with, played video games with on our parents' couches, got shit-faced together on bar stools and chased girls in our town. Now I was seeing the real person behind the mask.

* * * *

The night before my interview with the doctor, I woke up to the sound of Jake mumbling in his sleep. He kept repeating a word that sounded like "minnow."

In the morning, I told him what he'd said in his sleep. I wasn't prepared for the look on his face, as if I'd just exposed his darkest secret. He got angry, which I took for embarrassment, and headed for the shower. That's when I first noticed the owl tattoo on his back. I might be the last guy of my generation not to wear ink. The Gaelic cross and panther head on his shoulders seemed an odd combination, but the owl on his back was downright bizarre.

"Some owl, Jake," I said.

He was picking through his duffel bag of clothing.

He whipped around, startled; the look on his face was unlike any expression I'd seen except for the day we met up back home; it rotated from confused through surprised to hostile in a split-second. Then his face resumed the normal Jake-mask, all smiles and good cheer.

"I got it done in Jamaica a couple years ago. Hurt like hell."

It wasn't that cigar-box owl, or the friendly "wise owl" of TV commercials; it was a predator with its talons stretched out for a strike and those bulging, goggle eyes.

"Is it supposed to mean something to you?" I asked.

"Hell, I don't remember. I was blitzed," he said. "Let's get to work."

Back to it we went, with my ever-expanding mariner's vocabulary of terms like "pitch-poled," and mastering equations for a ship's capacity to "positive righting moment" and determining the "angle of vanishing stability."

That night, he turned in his bed to shut off the light and hesitated. He looked at me. I was exhausted from the endless question-answer routine and my hands were sore from that damned brick.

"That owl on my back—" he began.

"Whatever, I'm tired. Kill the light," I said. I was in no mood to talk about his stupid tattoo.

Ten seconds passed; then I heard his voice, low, as if speaking of a private joke. "It's the last thing a mouse in the forest sees."

* * * *

The doctor and his wife were a fit couple in their sixties. Both Nusbaums were gray-haired, attractive, and tanned from frequent voyages. My so-called exam went well. I was hired on the spot, Jake beaming beside me like a proud dad at a parent-teacher conference.

The spacious interior of the *Cassie*'s gleaming mahogany, her polished brightwork on deck, and the mix of ancient and gee-whiz technology in the cockpit made me feel like a cheap liar.

On our way to the motel to get our gear, I told Jake about my seasickness.

His eyes bugged. "Wh—what? What are you saying?"

The blood drained from his face; his stark reaction surprised me.

"I'd forgotten about it," I said meekly.

When I sailed all those long years ago, I used to get sea-sick in choppy waters coming down Lake Michigan on a short run from Lake Superior to South Chicago, the steamship's hold full of taconite. The water in the toilet bowl swirled from side to side as the roll and pitch of the ore boat made my meals in the galley come back. Climbing straight up from the bottom of the hold to the top of the hatch three stories high after the bulldozers and stevedores had finished scraping the hold clean, I gripped the rungs of the ladder in my thick gloves, too terrified to look down, fighting off nausea and dizziness, knowing that two feet of solid steel would be what I would hit if I let go. The *Col. James Pickands* was my last boat, and the memories of clinging to the dust-filled rungs of the vertical steel ladder came roaring back like a recurring nightmare.

"We'll get you medicine," Jake pronounced. That ended it, his buddy-face back in place.

* * * *

The Dramamine and Bonine never did work well enough to stabilize my floating equilibrium, but the elastic bands on my wrist somehow saved me. The hard part was avoiding Nusbaum on deck when my stomach was at its queasiest. I had to hustle on deck beside Jake working the ropes and sails. Staring at the horizon helped my equilibrium except when we were confined belowdecks in rough weather. I'll give Jake credit: he helped me with the rigging and other chores without making it obvious I was out of my element.

We were six days out and heading to port again, this time the Grenadines. I'd seen enough hurricane-ravaged islands by then to last me a lifetime. Guadeloupe and Dominica were stripped bare of foliage, winded-blasted houses left open to the sun, piles of debris everywhere, the people desperate, solemn, walking in single file or clusters down dirt roads staring ahead like zombies. We always stayed in port once the provisions were on board because it was too risky to venture far from the marina at night. A mixed blessing because time on shore was a relief to my tortured stomach and confused ear canals. I'd have sold my soul for a shot of whisky.

We watched the Nusbaums in their best tourist outfits head ashore in Carriacou.

"Kiss my ass," I said. "All I've done is vomit over the side whenever the old man isn't looking."

Carriacou was a nice change of pace, however. The people are a mix of Scottish and African ancestry. You see dark-skinned people with light eyes and wheat-blond hair. The waters are crystalline, the reefs pristine. We were anchored off Paradise Beach. One of the locals onshore was surrounded by tourists in fancy sun hats watching him build a boat in the traditional way he'd learned from his Scots grandfather in the village of Windward.

The Nusbaums gave us a few hours' shore leave. We strolled down the bustling streets of Hillsborough, the main tourists drag on the small island.

"Liquor, liquor everywhere, and not a drop to drink for us deck slaves."

Jake glared at me. He grabbed my bicep. His grip was hard; his forearms were all ropy muscle. "I told you the Nusbaums were teetotalers," he hissed. "One whiff of booze on our breaths and we'll be stranded here."

"Relax," I said. "I remember the deal." I pulled my arm free.

He recovered his temper in that rapid-fire way I'd seen before. "You have to admit one thing," he said. "Old lady Nusbaum is one hot-looking MILF."

Her cooking, however, left my stomach churning with acid. Bread helped soak up stomach acid but it was joyless eating. Jake ate enough for both of us and never put on a pound.

That evening, the Nusbaums returned with another couple and introduced us. They looked to be from the same income bracket as the Nusbaums. The husband was a Wall Street broker, balding and pudgy, mid-fifties; his wife must have been a real knockout in her youth. Curvy and leggy, exposing lots of deep-dish cleavage, she appeared on deck as gracefully as a deer fording a creek.

Down below, I asked Jake: "What's up with you?"

"What do you mean?"

"That guy and his trophy wife," I said. "You looked everywhere but at them when Nusbaum introduced us, like you were looking around for the lost head of John the Baptist."

I tried to lighten it up, but he reminded me of a meth freak back home, all twitchy nerves.

"You're full of shit," Jake replied.

"Nusbaum noticed it, too," I said.

"They're going with us to Aruba," he said.

"So frigging what? Nobody's going to deprive us of our berths down here. That second stateroom is big enough to park their his-and-hers Lambos."

"Go to sleep, Pete," Jake replied. "I'm beat to shit doing all your work for you."

That comment would have made sense any day on the water, but we had done nothing all day in port but boat-sit and cultivate our tans on deck. Bored, I cast a fishing line over the stern and hauled up a couple grunts and a hog fish that had strayed too far into the harbor.

* * * *

That night with all aboard, Jake had another nightmare. Just before dawn, he shot upright in his bunk talking a blue streak, unintelligible gibberish most of it, but it sounded urgent and mean, like a drill sergeant barking orders at recruits. A cobalt-blue sky leaked through the nearest porthole, still too early for the lemony shades the rising sun would cast over everything in the harbor.

My plan was to jump ship in Aruba. I'd had my bellyful of sailing under false pretenses, my nausea, but mostly Jake. My lack of seafaring skills annoyed him, but it didn't explain this rift in our friendship. That meant half-pay for the voyage—fine by me. They'd pick up another sailor in a busy place like Aruba. I wasn't leaving the Nusbaums or Jake in the lurch.

Sleep eluded me. My thoughts drifted in all directions, a few pleasant but some bitter—those memories we keep at bay until sleep overwhelms our defenses and they come flooding in like enemy soldiers at the gate. My senses seemed acutely aware: the typical night sounds like water lapping against the wharf, or the hull's gentle roll, swaying against the dock fenders, the piercing screech of a gull.

I looked over at Jake's bunk. He wasn't in it.

No big deal, I thought. *Off to the head for a piss.*

A noise, loud, just above the teak decking, like something heavy dropped amidships. Faint but discernible words—somebody speaking—*no, two voices speaking, one angry.* I placed the sound close to the galley.

I got up to investigate. I pulled on shorts and deck shoes and headed topside.

Nothing but the silhouettes of buildings against a lightening sky over the black water. I heard diesel engines start to life and saw the outlined shapes of men aboard nearby fishing boats moving tackle and preparing nets for the day's catch. No sign of Jake topside, however.

I hesitated to call out. My presence as a deckhand would have been unexpected anywhere near the captain's quarters. Certain parts of the vessel were off-limits to the hired help.

About to head back down, I turned when my right foot slid on some grease. Those teak decks were spit-shined to a polish and Captain Nusbaum was as fanatical about neatness as he must have been in the operating theater as a surgeon.

A woman's voice came through an open porthole. It sounded like moaning. I'd just avoided a catastrophic mistake, I thought; imagine barging in on a couple in bed amid their lovemaking? I smiled and went below to my bunk.

Jake was standing near my bunk.

"What's going on?"

He turned to face me in the dim light. The look on his face was like the night I discovered his owl tattoo. Owls are creatures of the night, swift and silent. The thought chilled me in the dawn light.

My brain worked on the puzzle: Jake standing by my bed, dressed in dark clothing from head to foot; his eyes wide open; his shirt front glistened.

That's when I noticed my own footprints behind me; my right shoe had left a foot imprint from the grease on deck moments ago…

Wait, that's not grease…

I put it all together too late. Whatever was in Jake's fist snapped out and struck me on the point of my jaw. It felt like steel.

* * * *

When I came to, we were moving over open water. Propped against the side of my bunk, my hands and feet were secured in nylon cuffs. My neck was secured by a rope to the bunk rail soldered to the deck flooring. Blood had dribbled down the front of my chest and dried. Two of my lower teeth were loose when I probed with my tongue.

Waves rolled beneath the boat. Even concussed, I knew Captain Nusbaum wasn't at the helm; with the inboard diesel running, I felt the prop cavitating in the steep waves.

The Nusbaums and their guests were either somewhere aboard and incapacitated like me—or Jake had stolen the boat and left them ashore. Had I said something that caused him to lash out?

Question without an answer. But I had to get free and find out; every instinct in me screamed danger. No one could steal a boat this big and expensive and expect to get away with it unless... Jake had been planning this for a long time. Somewhere in the back of my mind, Jake's muttered word clicked home: *Minnow. Mine now.* I was his trained monkey. I wondered if our meeting back home was an accident at all.

I sat there writhing in my bonds, my thoughts scrambled, when he appeared in the door.

"How 'bout a little stroll on deck?" were the first words out of his mouth.

"Jake, what the hell—"

"Shut up. I'm the captain now."

He pulled the retractable steel baton out of his belt and whipped it toward me at its full extension just an inch from my face. I thought of that owl again.

"Do something, anything, stupid and I won't hesitate," he said. "We cool?"

He told me how I should act once the restraints were removed. My hands remained cuffed. Jake the teacher, once again, explaining to a dimwitted student. Only this time he didn't need to cajole me into learning my lesson. The baton was back in his belt, but he showed me the short-barreled revolver. I knew he'd not hesitate to kill me and roll me over the side for chum.

"Brace yourself. You're going to see something," he said. "Don't go all girly."

It wasn't one thing; it was four of them.

Nusbaum, brave man, had died fighting. Arterial blood had sprayed the headboard behind him and dotted his dead wife with red freckles from her bare shoulders to her feet. Her nightgown was completely red below her neck; her open eyes stared at oblivion.

"Nusbaum didn't give me a choice," he said.

"Some choice," I muttered.

"Remember what I said," Jake replied.

My sea legs weren't used to the pitch and roll of a fast-moving sail-boat. The autopilot must have a bad angle on the incoming waves. Jake noticed the wobble in my legs as waves pounded the hull.

"I'll have to reset the autopilot," he said.

"Where are we going?"

"Not Aruba," he said. "Don't you worry about it."

"Where's the other couple?"

Jake retaliated fast with a sweeping leg kick that knocked me to the deck. I felt the barrel pressed hard into my temple. He said nothing but dug it into my skin, twisting it to leave a mark.

"That's twice," Jake said. "Third time means it's over. Understand?"

"I have to vomit," I said as matter-of-factly as I could manage.

He motioned to the starboard rail beyond salon. "I'll be right behind you with this." He grazed my cheek hard with the gunsight.

A ropy string of yellow bile was all I could manage.

"Get up," Jake said.

He jerked me away from the rail. With my buckling knees and my woozy head, I staggered down the deck weaving from side to side while he cursed me from behind and shoved the gun barrel into my ribs every time I slowed.

The stock broker and his wife were gagged, lying on deck bound by cuffs and secured to a coiled hawser by a pair of stainless steel "sea dogs," U-shaped bolts with a transom eye. Jake shoved me toward them and I fell to my knees. Both their heads turned to me, their eyes raking my face for some explanation. Two helpless strangers looking to me for answers to their fate.

The fact they were not bleeding gave me some hope until I turned my head and noticed the auxiliary anchor attached to the hawser.

O Jesus, merciful God—

Had there been anything left in my stomach, I would have heaved once more on the spot.

"Help me with them," Jake said. He held the gun to my forehead while he slit the cuffs.

"I—I won't do it, I can't do it—"

The barrel was jammed hard under my chin snapping my head back-wards.

"Last chance."

Gutless, terrified, I did it.

Jake directed me to grab the man's feet. I looked in his face, saw the pleading eyes; we set him down near the port bow. Then we placed his wife near his legs.

"Move back," Jake said.

Jake shoved me to the deck and placed the gun to the back of my head. "Do it!"

I didn't let myself think. I pushed, straining the anchor until it went over the side. The rope snapped taut. The man's body followed the anchor as if he were placed in a greased chute; her mouth gag slipped loose as he disappeared over the side. She gave out a long scream, a death yodel that made me feel as if ice had replaced my blood. The hellish noise died only when she hit the water after her husband.

They were gone… Just like that: they were gone.

Standing behind me, Jake said, "She's not a real blonde, you notice?"

The wind had blown her nightie up to her waist just before she disappeared.

I thought: *I might as well die now, too. Get it over with, you sick bastard.*

I tried to get to my feet, but I'd used every ounce of strength pushing the anchor. I stared at the waves, gray humps stretching to the horizon, dazed, gasping for air despite the headwind buffeting us.

I heard the words. I can't say I felt fear or panic then. I was drained of all feeling.

"So long, you loser."

The bullet that hit me felt like a Louisville slugger.

* * * *

Why Jake didn't roll me over the side then was a thought I wouldn't get to for a long time. I was gone like that couple I'd helped kill. I was as empty as a molecule in deep space. Hearing goes last; maybe it comes back first.

I remembered a thumping, waves smashing the portside hull. The *Cassie* was fighting a succession of big waves at an oblique angle. It'd take a tsunami to break a boat this size, but swells have to be only a third the ship's length to roll it. If the helmsman fails to keep the face of every wave from breaking as it encounters a vessel, where the energy is stored, that's bad news.

Jake had never figured on hijacking a luxury sailing yacht in the middle of a violent thunderstorm. The arrival of the couple back in Carriacou had forced his hand. I came to under a black sky, the clouds' bellies spoked by jagged flashes of lightning; the pelting rain washed my face of blood and revived me. I crawled like a baby down Nusbaum's beautiful deck, my progress mere inches at a time.

I was disoriented from pain and loss of blood. The slug must have ricocheted off my skull. Forks of lightning allowed me to see enough to work myself to a position on all fours without tipping over on the rolling deck. Our speed had slowed but the winds grew more intense. Jake must be steering from the cockpit to keep the *Cassie* oriented to the waves.

I reached the helm. Jake couldn't steer and trim sails at the same time; he was fighting to stabilize the vessel's center of gravity from the waves hitting broadside. If I hadn't come to when I did, I would have been swept over the side. Salt water burned my eyes. I shook water off like a dog and kept moving, guided by a single thought in my limbic brain: *kill*.

I slithered behind the T-shaped cockpit well next to the companionway sill and crouched low. Jake was in front, manhandling the wheel, trying to overcome the heeling caused by too much wind in the sails. With no way to spill the wind in the sails, he had no choice but to head right into it and risk rolling. All his attention was focused on the task of steering, staring past the coachroof into blackness. Lightning flashes would have exposed me had he not been engaged in a life-and-death struggle with the forces of nature.

A bolt of lightning hit the water off to starboard and lit the entire sky and every inch of the boat and the churning waves. Lying on the seatback couch was the steel baton he'd used on me.

I sucked in my breath and stood up, throwing myself forward; in my motion, I swept the baton off the couch and in one motion had it extended.

The crashing waves and howling wind muffled the sound of Jake's head cracking open. He dropped straight down like a puppet with its strings cut.

I didn't stop to look at what I'd done. The *Cassie* slewed and if I hadn't grabbed the wheel when I did, the next wave would have rolled her over with no chance of righting us. By the time the storm broke, and the winds had calmed, my arms were lead. I was on autopilot myself, a body working through adrenalin and a will not to die after being resurrected on deck.

Just when I thought the worst was over, when the winds were putting less pressure on the sails, a rogue wave rolled us. It's one thing to memorize a term like "vanishing stability," it's another thing to avoid it from happening in reality.

The stabilizing physics of the massive keel jutting out of the water like a beached whale kept me from drowning in that sea. I had no idea where we were. Overhead, an overcast pewter-gray sky with scudding clouds obscured everything. The sea and sky merged in one gauzy blur.

Still, I was alive. Wounded and nauseated to the marrow of my being—but alive.

* * * *

I drifted on the current clinging to the mainsail mast, moving farther toward the end as the *Cassie* took on more water. I must have been dreaming at some point, fading in and out of consciousness. Waterlogged, thirsty, badly sunburned on my face, neck, and hands by the end of the second day of drifting.

Toward sundown of the third day, a shark fin appeared out of nowhere. It was a big one, maybe ten feet from snout to tail judging by the apple-green silhouette beneath the water's surface. Thrashing in the water was a dinner bell to a shark. He cruised back and forth closing the distance each time. All I could do was try to keep the mast between him and me, a dangerous game of tag. How long that went on I can't remember. Painful as drowning would be, I preferred it to being eaten alive by a five-hundred-pound killing machine.

When the shark finally went away, I sobbed, adding my tears to the ocean. The salt water helped keep my wound from infecting. Half my face was swollen, and one eye was closed. I was sleepy all the time and lost my grip on the mast and had to swim to it. My fuzzy brain tossed up a memory: a painting from one of Cindy's coffee table books: a slave sits on a dismasted, rudderless boat surrounded by sharks.

* * * *

I was close to death, they told me later, belaboring the obvious. A sportfishing boat from Basseterre rescued me. Jake must have intended to find some cove in St. Kitts and Nevis in the West Indies and lay low while he disguised the *Cassiopeia* before sailing on.

I spent four days in a hospital treated for the gunshot wound and a bad staph infection. When my fever hit one-oh-five, they induced a coma. Surgeons sawed out a portion of my skull bone to allow for brain swelling. They gave me antibiotics for Bilharzia, a tropical disease caused by flatworm parasites.

I got so tired of telling the police authorities the same story, especially to the FBI, that I could have recited it backwards. Jake's shark-mauled torso washed ashore on a reef near Dominica three days after I left the hospital. The bodies of the Nusbaums and their guests were never recovered.

Three polygraphs, which I volunteered to take, all showed deception in the same place: *Did I have anything to do with the deaths of Mr. and Mrs.—?* I still can't say their names. In the end, there wasn't enough evidence for a grand jury to return a true bill. I returned home, courtesy of the embassy in Charlotte Amalie.

People avoid me. They've heard the rumors. The local newspaper stopped sending a reporter to hassle me. I've developed bleeding ulcers and so drinking anything stronger than green tea will leave me doubled over. I have blinding headaches. I work three days a week at a car wash on Depot Road. The teenagers I work with mock me behind my back. I've caught them imitating my palsied hands. The tremors are psychosomatic, they tell me.

I used those hands to send two innocent people to a cruel death. Certain images are scored into my brain like the wind lifting her chemise exposing her legs to the open sea with her luxuriant hair tumbling around her face as she follows her husband into the dark depths.

That bullet came to rest near the stump of my limbic brain. One more millimeter and I'd have died instantly. Even so, it created havoc with some of my senses. I salivate like a Komodo Dragon. The kids at the car wash find my uncontrollable drooling hilarious. I've developed Morgellons, a weird neurological disease where red and blue "fibers" grow out of the skin, which eventually leads to permanent mental and neurological deterioration.

I avoid water. I won't drive down streets where I can see Lake Erie. In mythology, Queen Cassiopeia herself made a single thoughtless mistake by bragging that her beauty surpassed the Nereids and so displeased these sea nymphs they appealed to god of the sea for revenge. I'll never be right again.

I learned more about Jake's betrayal. My ex confirmed it the day I showed up at her house, the one we had built together for our future. Before she slammed the door in my face, she told me she and Jake had been lovers long before the divorce. On the day I met him in the street, he was coming from her place.

I staggered down the sidewalk, going nowhere, my heart aching and my head buzzing with the noise of a thousand flies. The first words Jake said to me when we met up were *Go to hell*. How was I to know he was the demon who was going to escort me there?

✗

Robb T. White was born, raised, and still lives in Northeastern Ohio. He writes noir, crime, and hardboiled stories featuring series character Thomas Haftmann, the latest a short-story collection: *Thomas Haftmann, Private Eye*. A pair of crime novels are *When You Run with Wolves* and *Waiting on a Bridge of Maggots* (2015). *Dangerous Women: Stories of Crime, Mystery, and Mayhem* (2017) collects short stories and a novella. Crowood Press recently published White's latest work: *Perfect Killer*.

BEYOND A REASONABLE DOUBT
Ashley Lynch-Harris

Mr. Henry Cubbage was a portly fellow, a man of self-indulgence and strict routine. After having served 67 years in that drafty law office with those wretched wooden chairs and seemingly endless piles of papers, he retired and adapted quite easily to his new position in life.

Sinking into his leather chair at the Empire Club, with a bottle of his favorite port, and being waited on by his usual server, Mr. Cubbage sighed happily as he unwrapped his wool scarf from around his neck and sifted his pudgy fingers through a box of truffles.

"Mm, yes... quite nice, quite nice indeed," he murmured.

Yes, Mr. Cubbage was a thoroughly satisfied man, and as the sun descended on the small town of Westend Bay and the fireplace warmed his bones, he resembled a large toad peering contentedly ahead through narrow, drowsy eyes.

Following Mr. Cubbage's line of sight, one would find that it was settled in the general direction of the club's main entrance where Mr. Hensley, the doorman, was posted. Presently, he was opening the door for a tall woman with gaunt cheeks and thin lips. Her hair was simply styled and a dull gray-brown color. Her dress, which was a faded shade of blue, matched her eyes and hung loosely from her body.

From across the room, a tiny crinkle formed in Mr. Cubbage's brow as he caught glimpse of the woman's face from over the doorman's shoulder.

How peculiar... thought Mr. Cubbage as his droopy eyelids rose. *Could that be...* Mr. Cubbage frowned. *Yes, I'm almost certain it is... from the William Lawson Case. Why has she returned, I wonder?*

The doorman, in Mr. Cubbage's estimation, seemed unaffected by the woman with whom he was speaking—as though he didn't recognize her, however, one could never tell with Mr. Hensley. He was a lanky gentleman with a quiet, formal disposition and keen eye. His expression was always one of indifference and he spoke in such a detached, impersonal way that club members felt assured of his discretion.

Such a blasted hard man to read! thought Mr. Cubbage irritably.

Mr. Cubbage stiffened as the woman suddenly pushed past Mr. Hensley to search the main room before the doorman swiftly managed to remove her from their sitting area.

My, my! thought Mr. Cubbage as the woman stormed away. Mr. Hensley, of course, returned calmly to his post, his expression just as wooden as before.

That man must play poker, decided Mr. Cubbage. *I can't tell one way or the other if he recognized her—if he realized that woman is a murderer.*

* * * *

"If you would pass the salt—" remarked Mr. Cubbage to his nephew from across the dinner table.

Tim Downing cast a disapproving glance at his uncle. His uncle visited once a week for dinner, and once a week they had some discussion concerning his health.

"That is your second helping, and the doctor said—" started Tim.

"Oh! Never mind what the doctor said!"

Mr. Cubbage always did find his nephew a bit tiresome. Always so sensible! Why couldn't he leave a man alone to live as he pleases?

Tim was an intelligent man in his mid-forties with a deep voice and friendly smile. He was smiling now.

"Mother called me today—" started Tim again.

"Oh! You're relentless!" interjected Mr. Cubbage once more. "That sister of mine doesn't know a thing about it. Cholesterol this. Blood pressure that. I'm perfectly well, I tell you."

From behind a book rose the doubtful eyes of a young woman in her early 20's. She too was sharing dinner with her father, Tim, and granduncle, Mr. Cubbage, but Mr. Cubbage, never having been very good with children or "variations thereof," as he puts it (being that a 20-year-old was hardly considered a child), never did know what to say to them. Tim's daughter, Audrey, was always gracious in this regard and carried a book to read during her granduncle's visits, and he had become quite accustomed to her quiet presence. She was respectful, intelligent, and well-mannered—almost as though she weren't even there at all, a wonderful relief for Mr. Cubbage.

Abandoning his quest for salt, Mr. Cubbage cleared his throat and remarked on the events of his day.

"A curious thing happened at the club today," he began. "A woman visited…"

"Hmm, yes," murmured Tim as he finished the last bit of his mashed potatoes. "That *is* something—being a men's only club."

"Stop with the condescension, Timothy. My life isn't all that dull," snapped Mr. Cubbage. "Let me finish."

Audrey smiled secretly from behind her book.

"The woman who came to visit is a *murderer*—she murdered her husband, William Lawson, several years ago, but was never convicted."

This time Timothy's expression was one of genuine interest, and Mr. Cubbage took a sip of his wine, allowing himself a moment to relish his small victory.

"I don't understand, Uncle," inquired Tim. "If she was never convicted, how can you be so convinced she murdered her husband?"

"The details of the case—that's how. The details almost prove that she did it, but she managed to get off."

"Almost?" asked Audrey, startling Mr. Cubbage.

Audrey peered at Mr. Cubbage through light brown eyes as she lowered her book. Her mustard yellow cardigan and dark auburn hair reminded Mr. Cubbage of a fall morning.

"Er—yes…" Mr. Cubbage sniffed heartily and replied. "I'll explain then—from the beginning."

Mr. Cubbage folded his napkin and thought for a moment.

"Yes," he said slowly. "There were four key people involved in the case: Mr. William Lawson, a fairly successful business man; Gwen Lawson, his wife; Michael Combs, a fellow businessman and friend of Mr. Lawson; and Helen Combs, the friend's wife." Mr. Cubbage scratched at his round belly, a habit he had when mulling things over. "I believe," he said cautiously, "the Lawsons were married only a year or two…"

"No children?" asked Tim.

"No—no kids," confirmed Mr. Cubbage. "But that's for the best, I'd say," he continued. "As I already mentioned, Mr. Lawson was murdered, and it occurred on the night that Mr. and Mrs. Lawson held a dinner party with Michael and Helen Combs."

Tim leaned back and listened intently.

"Dinner started with fresh salad," Mr. Cubbage explained. "Mrs. Lawson kindly offered to serve the salad and started around the table, dishing out her husband's first. As she moved to her guests, she tripped on the rug and the entire bowl of salad scattered across the floor. Of course, she apologized, embarrassed, but mistakes happen. The guests insisted Mr. Lawson enjoy his salad even though they didn't have any. Being that it was a very casual occasion, they proceeded with the rest of the dinner in which they all ate the same thing, which exception of Mr. Lawson, of course, who also had a salad.

"Dinner concluded about an hour later, and Mr. Lawson remarked to his wife that he didn't feel very well. Apparently, he became weak and unable to move. His wife called the doctor (not immediately, mind you—claiming she didn't realize how bad his condition was at first), and within several hours he was dead. The death, of course, was treated as suspicious. After all, it was entirely unexpected, and although Mr. Lawson had not taken out life insurance, it was discovered later that he had invested a large sum of money into several pieces of diamond jewelry. If the wife had killed her husband, that was considered a possible and likely motive."

"And what of Mr. and Mrs. Combs—the Lawson's dinner guests?"

"Not much there," answered Mr. Cubbage. "The business friend of his wasn't a competitor. He didn't gain from Mr. Lawson's death, and the wife barely knew him. There wasn't any motive."

"So, police were pretty sure the wife was guilty?" asked Tim.

"That's right. An autopsy was performed, and it was discovered that the salad was actually made with 'Fool's Parsley'—it's a plant that looks a lot like parsley, but it's poisonous."

"Terrible," murmured Tim. "But it seems fairly obvious, doesn't it?"

"That's what everyone else said," agreed Mr. Cubbage. "The wife must have killed her husband for the diamonds. Prosecutors, however, knew that the defense would argue that many people have died by mistakenly eating 'Fools Parsley.'"

"Yes," conceded Tim. "But the way she dropped the salad seems a bit too suspicious."

Mr. Cubbage shrugged. "Again, I agree with you, but *technically* both truly could have been accidental, and you could sway a jury to agree if you went about it the right way. So, they really needed a strong case to make this murder charge stick."

"I'm assuming they intended to play up the motive of the valuable diamonds?" asked Tim.

Mr. Cubbage reclined in his chair and crossed his arms over his belly. A smug expression swept across his face as he replied:

"Mr. Lawson stored his diamonds in a safe," explained Mr. Cubbage, "and only his wife knew the location—it was *very* well hidden in their house. You either knew where it was or you didn't. There was no stumbling upon it. After a sufficient interval of time and of course a decent grief-stricken display at the funeral, Mrs. Lawson decided to go through her husband's things." Mr. Cubbage lowered his chin and peered at his nephew knowingly. "She started with the safe."

"I had a feeling…" remarked Tim.

"But when she opened the safe," Mr. Cubbage went on, "she found that the jewels were gone. Stolen! Just the empty jewelry boxes were left."

"The plot thickens," said Tim cheerfully.

"To make matters worse for Mrs. Lawson, the town had already convicted her in their minds and made sure she knew it. You can imagine the tension. It wasn't long before rumors were floating around that the police were planning on charging her for the murder."

"My, what a gossip you are, Uncle!" exclaimed Tim as he shifted in his chair and made himself more comfortable.

"Oh, shut up, Timothy!" grumbled Mr. Cubbage who considered not finishing his story just to spite his nephew, but he was too committed now to stop. "Now, where was I?"

"The jewels were stolen," replied Audrey, her voice clear and fresh.

Goodness! thought Mr. Cubbage with a start. *How do I so easily forget that child is there?*

"Yes, thank you…" Mr. Cubbage gave a dry cough and went on. "The prosecutors suspected that in anticipation of being charged for her husband's murder, Mrs. Lawson made up the stolen jewelry excuse to make it appear as though she wasn't gaining by her husband's death—soften up the jury, I suppose."

Tim considered his uncle's remarks and nodded. "Everything they have against her really was just circumstantial."

"Precisely," said Mr. Cubbage. "As a result, the police continued to dig deeper. They couldn't afford to charge her with so little to go on. Eventually the phone records revealed that one number appeared several times over the few months preceding the murder. It was the number of the Empire Club—*my* club. Someone had been speaking with Mrs. Lawson regularly and that someone was obviously a member."

Tim scratched at his chin as he considered this new bit of information.

"Interesting," he said. "Interesting, indeed."

Tim suddenly straightened. "Uncle, when did you say you became a member?"

Mr. Cubbage snorted in contempt and stood, walking toward the fireplace.

"Do you want to hear the rest of the details or not?" he asked.

Tim laughed heartily as he and Audrey joined Mr. Cubbage by the fire.

"We do, and I'm sorry," said Tim. "It really is very interesting."

Tim and Audrey took a seat on the couch as Mr. Cubbage remained standing beside the fire. His round belly cast a shadow across the wool rug and the warmth of the fire improved his temperament enough to continue.

"Like I said, a member of the club was obviously in regular contact with Mrs. Lawson. The police made inquiries and discovered that it was a fellow by the name of Brennan Davis. He admitted that they had started an affair a few months earlier. The club seemed the safest place from which to call."

"So, perhaps the lover managed to switch the salads and maybe the wife didn't even know about it. Her tripping really was pure dumb luck."

"No," replied Mr. Cubbage, shaking his head. "If he killed Mrs. Lawson's husband out of some sort of misguided love, I would think he would have told her about the salad. If not, it would have been too risky. She could have eaten it and died as well."

"Okay," said Tim. "Then they were both in on it."

Mr. Cubbage shook his head even more adamantly. "He might have known about the murder plot, but he didn't actually help to carry it out. Mr. Hensley, our doorman, confirmed that Mr. Davis was at the club the entire evening, and he was sure he never saw him leave during the time the murder took place."

"But the lover must be involved somehow!" exclaimed Tim. "They always are. I bet he stole the diamonds. Lovers tell each other secrets. Mrs. Lawson probably told him about the diamonds when they concocted their plan to kill the husband, and he double-crossed her."

"The police thought so, too," said Mr. Cubbage. "The police kept an eye on them both for a time—hoping they could find who would lead them to the diamonds and build the stronger case they'd been hoping for. Unfortunately, nothing came of it. They searched both their houses and didn't find anything. They searched everywhere Mrs. Lawson and Mr. Davis frequented and even places they didn't but had been seen. They searched the club—nothing. Finally," said Mr. Cubbage, throwing up his hands, "they went ahead and charged Mrs. Lawson with murder. They were playing on a hunch because they knew no one else could have possibly done it."

"But with almost no *real* evidence," said Tim thoughtfully, "the jury would have essentially been guessing if she were guilty of intentionally murdering her husband or if it really was just a terrible accident."

Mr. Cubbage nodded. "But the key is that the jury must be convinced 'beyond a reasonable doubt' that Mrs. Lawson murdered her husband— that no other logical explanation exists. With the evidence presented (or lack thereof), the jury, in good conscience, could not say they felt that beyond a reasonable doubt she was guilty of intentionally murdering her husband."

"So, she went free—to be with her lover and probably retrieve her diamonds she has stashed somewhere," said Tim.

"I imagine so," said Mr. Cubbage with a firm nod.

"No," said Audrey.

Both Mr. Cubbage and Tim turned to the young woman, slightly taken aback not so much by her simple remark, but rather the tone in which she made it.

"No what, Audrey?" asked her father. "You sound quite definite about something."

"Your conclusion…" A faint hue of red tinged Audrey's cheeks. "I'm sorry, that was rude of me, but I just mean to say that Mrs. Lawson did not run off with her lover, and they certainly didn't live happily ever after with the diamonds."

Mr. Cubbage laughed. "How preposterous. I told you all the facts."

"Precisely," said Audrey. "That's how I know that Mrs. Lawson did not run off with her lover or the diamonds."

"What do you think happened, Audrey?" encouraged her father, curious.

"First," she began, "I think Mrs. Lawson did kill her husband. She was having an affair—she obviously didn't love him, diamonds were to be gained, and the salad situation was, I agree, a bit too coincidental. Of course, I also agree that the jury had no choice but to rule 'not guilty.' She was smart though, using 'Fool's Parsley.' Very smart, in fact. The possibility of the poison having been a mistake presented a definite gray area, and one can cast quite a bit of doubt with gray areas. Had she used a clearly villainous poison like arsenic or strychnine then there'd be no question—but a leafy salad…." Audrey shrugged.

"But now to the point of her lover and the diamonds," Audrey went on. "It's ironic. She may have gotten rid of her husband, but because the diamonds really were stolen, she ultimately lost her lover. It was a disappointment to lose valuable diamonds, of course, but the real issue is that each suspected the other of having stolen the diamonds for themselves! Now, I suppose I'm a bit young to know much about relationships, but I imagine it's rather hard to have a relationship based on trust when you met as adulterers and plotted to kill the man to whom she had originally vowed to love for the rest of her life."

"That is a valid point," agreed Tim, amused.

"Right—so these once-lovers who really didn't steal the diamonds wondered if the other secretly had. They certainly can't live happily ever after with that hanging over their heads and they part ways. The fact that Mrs. Lawson returned looking for Mr. Davis at the club confirmed that they had not been together."

"That's true, I suppose," said Mr. Cubbage, "and I know that Mr. Davis hasn't been a member of the club since the scandal. Had they been together all that time, she would have known that."

"Exactly," said Audrey.

"I can also tell you," added Mr. Cubbage, "she did not look like she had been living a luxurious life. If she did think Mr. Davis had the diamonds, she probably came back because she needed help financially. She looked a bit desperate as she searched for him. He might have been a last resort."

"But how do you know one of them didn't steal the diamonds?" asked Tim.

"Yes," said Mr. Cubbage. "How can you be sure about that?"

"Oh, that's because the doorman, Mr. Hensley, had stolen them," said Audrey.

Stunned, Mr. Cubbage stammered in response:

"I'm—I'm sorry. What do you mean *Mr. Hensley* stole the diamonds? That's ridiculous!"

"Why?" asked Audrey.

Mr. Cubbage was dumbfounded.

"Because he just couldn't have… wouldn't have," he mumbled feebly. "There would be no reason—"

"No reason?" countered Audrey, surprised. "Those diamonds could have been worth hundreds of thousands of dollars for all we know. Even thousands of dollars of diamonds might have been worth stealing to him."

"Okay, fine," said Mr. Cubbage taking a seat across from Audrey. "Tell me how a simple doorman went about all this."

Audrey smiled. "And *that's* how he did it. If you'll excuse my saying so, Uncle, but I've noticed that your perception of people is not uncommon. You asked me how a 'simple' doorman could go about stealing valuable diamonds. Doormen, cashiers, servers… these positions are often considered menial, and it seems to me that some people impose the status of one's position onto the person as a whole—as though it sums them up in entirety."

"Well… I only meant…" mumbled Mr. Cubbage.

"Oh, I'm not judging," continued Audrey. "My point is just that these are the same people who often go unnoticed. Young people, for instance, are extremely observant and clever, generating significant ideas that are sometimes more readily dismissed simply because of their age. Or, like in this case, a group of private club members may find themselves speaking freely in front of a doorman because his knowing details of their lives seems inconsequential to them. He is *only* a doorman. Combine these perceptions with the discreet atmosphere created in a private members club and you have someone like Mr. Davis who felt comfortable making frequent calls from there to Mrs. Lawson. As already discussed, lovers tell each other everything—adulterous lovers, especially, I expect."

Audrey was thoughtful for a moment, remarking more to herself than anyone else: "I imagine," she considered slowly, "adulterers sharing their deepest secrets truly solidifies for them the depth of their love—and I bet it even helps comfort the more guilt-ridden individuals in justifying their actions."

"Aw, that is an interesting notion, Audrey," said Tim. "They probably tell themselves, 'look how my marriage pales in comparison to this deep relationship I have with my adulterous partner.'"

Mr. Cubbage cleared his throat.

"Yes—yes, I agree. Very interesting," he mumbled, "but back to Mr. Hensley…"

"Oh, of course!" Heat rose in Audrey's cheeks. "As I was saying, I believe Mrs. Lawson revealed the location of the safe to her lover, and Mr. Hensley overheard Mr. Davis discussing it during one of the many phone calls he made to Mrs. Lawson. Mr. Hensley took advantage of the opportunity. Before Mrs. Lawson or Mr. Davis knew it, Mr. Hensley took the diamonds right out from under their noses."

"Incredible, Audrey," said Tim. "Well done! It does make sense!"

Audrey's cheeks warmed again, but this time she was feeling deeply gratified.

"Really, young lady," said Mr. Cubbage. "We really should talk more often."

Ashley Lynch-Harris is the author of *The Hotel Westend*, a novel Publishers Weekly has described as "a charming homage to the classic mystery…" She is an honors graduate of the University of South Florida and lives in Tampa with her husband, Alex. For more information, please visit www.AshleyLynchHarris.com.

THE TARGET
Charlie Hughes

I nod at Sandra and she smiles, wiggling her fingers at me from behind the window. She thinks I use the box for my business, a non-existent tech company just off Old Street.

This is my seventh checkpoint in sixteen years. Manchester, São Paulo, Birmingham, Athens, Kiev and Edinburgh have all been home. I've got one responsibility each day. Rain, wind or shine, I check the postal box.

The room is too bright, the tube lighting hissing above my head. The walls are covered with gray metal post boxes, numbered one to five hundred. I approach box 323 and open it with my card.

Inside, there's a large brown envelope.

I shouldn't get this shiver of anticipation, I know. I should not be smiling. But you've got to understand, when a man is this good at something, one of the absolute best, he needs to let it show.

* * * *

My little brother could see it.

As kids, we lived in a mobile home parked on farmland next to a small Warwickshire town. Mum left when we were young, I was eight and Joey four. The old man worked on building sites when he was sober and served behind the bar of a local pub when he wasn't.

Life was tough, particularly at school, where Joey and I were tarred with the 'gyppo' brush.

But there were good times too. The farmer was a kind man who took pity on us. He brought milk and cuts of meat when he had them to spare, and he gave Joey and I the run of the place. Six hundred acres of fields and hills with the river Stour running through the middle of it all. We grew up fishing that river, playing hide and seek in the woods and building dens in the trees.

One autumn day, I couldn't have been more than ten years old, we explored the big barn, west of the farmhouse. We knew we weren't supposed to, but that was part of the attraction. I remember Joey jumping into the hay pile and screaming when two mice scurried out from underneath.

He calmed down and we climbed the ladder into the loft. To our delight, we found a treasure trove of old tools and other farm junk. We messed around with them until Joey looked behind a pile of firewood stacked in the corner.

"Hey, Danny. Come and look," he said.

I went over. At Joey's feet was a cat lying on its side and six tiny kittens trying to get to their mother's milk. It didn't look like they were having much success. The kittens were frail and sluggish. Their mother was still, taking deep slow breaths, its eyes glazed.

"What do we do? Tell the farmer?" Joey asked.

"How'll we explain finding them?" I said.

The cat let out a long, low-pitched whine of pure agony.

Joey's lips shook. "It's real bad for the mum, Danny. What'll we do?" He did his best to hold back the tears.

"It's okay," I said, and went back to the junk. I emptied one of the wooden trays and passed it to Joey. "Put the little ones in this and take them outside. I'll take care of their mum."

"How?" he asked.

I looked at him for a short while, unsure if I should tell him. "Just get the little ones outside."

He picked up the kittens, placed them in the tray and carried them down the ladder.

When he was gone, I knelt down by that big moggy and lifted its head in my hand. I can still see her eyes now, panic and desperation all rolled into one. She began to let out another one of those awful moans.

Before the sound could rise, I snapped her neck.

* * * *

I get out of the lift and enter my penthouse apartment. The place is immaculate. I have a cleaning company come in twice a week and spruce up the place from top to bottom.

It's open plan with a mezzanine for the two bedrooms. Seven hundred square feet of luxury fittings, a huge earthstone kitchen, ultra HD home cinema and Bose SR sound system. Since I moved in two years ago, the cleaners and I are the only people to set foot inside.

I make myself coffee and settle on the sofa to read. Inside the envelope is a twelve-page dossier.

The top page is standard format, *"Top Secret, Level 7 Clearance only"* emblazoned across the top.

Targets: Bryce Martenson and Stephen Rodrigo (NC)

> *Required outcome: Termination*
> *Location: Targets travel from Moscow to Argentina on 17-02-17*
>   *(full flight details in appendix A). They have a one day stop-*
>   *over in Madrid en route, staying at the Ritz (Plaza de la*
>   *Lealtad. Room 327.)*
> *Method: Any means necessary.*
> *Cover: Scene must look like a disturbed robbery.*

Next to the word "robbery", a handwritten note is inserted. "*Same as Milan '06.*"

It is Westland's handwriting, my MI6 handler. In Milan, Phillips and I had waited in the hotel room of an oil Sheikh and his wife. The guy was siphoning money off from his business interests to fund Al-Qaeda operations in Iraq. But Westland was mis-remembering. We didn't make it look like a robbery. I mutilated the bodies to fit with a series of mafia hits.

"Same as Milan." I say. "Prick."

On the next page are three photographs of the same man. In two of them he is chubby-faced, walking down the street, unaware of being photographed. In the third, he is younger and slimmer, smiling for a passport picture.

> *Bryce Martenson is a UK national, genius hacker and traitor. Born in Salford, Lancs, he studied Programming at Cambridge. He was thrown out and arrested in his second year for taking down his college server and wiping their financial records. On his release from a six month stretch, he set up his own tech consulting company: Bitlife PLC.*
>
> *Martenson operated an above-the-line consultancy but secured financial success through illegal corporate hacking and cyber-attacks, funded by unscrupulous rivals. As the business grew, numerous attempts were made by the Serious Fraud Office to seek convictions and close him down. In 2010, when the net was finally closing, Martenson travelled to Serbia, ostensibly on holiday with his wife (Stephanie Rodrigo) and his newborn child.*
>
> *All three disappeared off the grid and didn't show up again until 2011. Operatives identified Martenson meeting with Russian FSB agents in Moscow and tracked him and his family to a luxury complex in the center of the city. Since that time, it has become clear Martenson's expertise is a central cog in the Russian cyber terrorism operation. His involvement has been verified in attacks on the London Olympics, US and UK elections and a variety of other highly disruptive attacks on the institutions of the British State.*

More information than they usually give. I don't distinguish on the grounds of motive, but it feels like they're making more effort than usual.

Now for Stephen Rodrigo, the NC, necessary collateral. I'm guessing a family member from the wife's side who helped to bring them over, FSB agent.

I flip the page.

Staring back at me is a picture of a boy. Six years old, maybe seven.

* * * *

Snapping a cat's neck doesn't turn you into a killer. But it started something: the first time I experienced the power, the raw, instinctual freedom the act bestows.

Joey could see the change in me and it concerned him. The fun went out of our games. We stopped our imaginary adventures in the woods and I lost the patience for fishing. I spent more time on my own, walking the hills and woods looking for prey. I bought a sling shot from a mail order catalogue and used it on birds, rabbits and squirrels on the farm.

It went on like that for a while—the two of us drifting apart, the older we got, the harder Dad drank. I hung out with some of the tougher kids from school and got into a few scrapes with the police. Social services hovered around for a while, threatening to take us into care if Dad didn't get his act together. Things were getting low and the twelve-year-old me did not understand how to stop the slide.

Then the snow came. Six days of heavy snowfall was unheard of in the midlands, but it just wouldn't stop. People round town had smiles on their faces, amused at the "extreme" weather hitting our sleepy town.

For the first time in a year, Joey and I went out into the fields together, making snowmen and chucking snowballs. Something about that great blanket of white seemed to snap me out of my dark mood and reminded me of how much fun I could have with my little brother.

We made an igloo and jumped into the drifts. One time, even Dad came out with us for a snowball fight. For me, it felt like a release of pressure.

It happened on the second day of the thaw.

Joey wanted to go sledging. It wasn't my idea. I told him the snow was getting thin and it wouldn't be much fun. We had this green plastic thing that dad brought home a few days before. God knows how he'd got hold of it, but I doubt it was paid for.

To my surprise, the hills were still slick. We picked out a few good runs, but we both knew it would be faster further west, on the bank of the

Stour.

I took the first go and stopped ten meters before the bank. When I stood up from the sledge, I looked down into the half-frozen river. What would it be like? What would it feel like to keep going and descend into the ice and water?

I turned around and looked up at my little brother. He was jumping up and down, excited at how fast I'd gone. I dragged the sledge back up to the top and let him climb inside. If I close my eyes now, I can still feel my fingers pressing onto the back of his waxy Parka jacket. I can see his little hands holding tight to the thin rope.

"You ready?" I said.

"Go, Danny. Let me go."

He didn't ask me to push him, he asked me to let him go. So why did I do it? I propelled him forwards, my hands still on his back. I told myself it would be more fun, that he would want to go faster.

Then I stopped, and I watched Joey fly down the hill. At first I could hear cries of joy, but as he approached the bottom of the hill, they stopped. He could see what I could see: the river getting too close, too fast.

All he had to do was tip the sledge over. It would've been easy. Tip it over and get a face full of snow, maybe a couple of bruises. But he kept going.

I didn't move until I knew he was going over, I sprinted down the hill, falling over several times as I went. By the time I reached the river bank, all I could see was the green sledge, upright, floating away to the east. Joey was nowhere.

I should have dived in. I should have tried to save him.

I stood still, watching ice and dirty water carry the sledge away.

* * * *

I've never asked for a face-to-face before.

They pay us the money and they give us the jobs, but as soon as your behavior becomes "disruptive," you're on borrowed time. I have known three associates, two of whom I considered friends, who were involuntarily retired due to behavioral difficulties. And when I say retired, I don't mean they got a pension and a carriage clock.

So there are certain rules it makes sense to follow: Never forget to check your box, don't hang out with any suspect persons (which is pretty much anybody in my book) and above all, do not ask too many questions. Operational detail is fine. Those little packs they leave for us are usually full of holes. Flight times, known associates, I even had one which left out the description and photographs of the target. When that happens, you book time on a secure line with your handler and the questions get answered.

Issues arise when you ask the 'why' question. Never question their motives. To do so is to question their authority. They have limited respect for us. We are killers and they bow to our usefulness, but we are not permitted to second guess decisions made by important people not just higher up the food chain, but at the very top.

So I thought long and hard before I made the call and booked this meeting. I'm sat in the lobby of a budget hotel on the Euston Road in central London.

A man in an inexpensive gray suit arrives to collect me and we travel up to the meeting room in silence. When I enter, James Westland sits behind a desk, pages of notes spread in front of him. This is only the third time I have met him. The first was on a US helicopter extracting me from Southern Syria. He needed an urgent debrief on my operations. The last was in a hotel similar to this one for a psych evaluation.

He is twelve types of arsehole rolled into human form.

Westland neither looks up nor speaks as I sit down in the chair opposite him. The gray suit takes a seat behind me.

After a predictable pause he says, "So what's this all about, Jenson?"

"The kid," I say. "You want me to kill a kid, and I need a better reason than 'necessary collateral.'"

"You don't need reasons, you need to do as you're fucking told." Finally, the prick looks up from his notes.

"I need more. He's seven, for Christ's sake. *Seven*."

He exhales. "The minor goes everywhere with him. Martenson has full Russian citizenship and so does his son."

"And?"

"So we can't leave witnesses and we can't adopt a Russian child into the loving arms of the British state without a diplomatic headache."

"So we murder a child, to save us the hassle?"

"*We* don't. *You* do. And nobody is any the wiser." He smirks at me in what he believes is a conciliatory gesture. It makes me want to tear his arms off.

He goes on. "This has been signed off at the highest level."

"This isn't right."

Westland snaps back. "Do I need to be concerned about you? Do I need to think about a Jenson retirement plan?"

I am silent for a few seconds, shocked that he's played this card so early. "You don't need to consider that. I was just—"

"Just what? You are questioning the chain of command. You are presuming to make moral judgements about what is and is not necessary to protect the interests of this country."

"I needed to be sure this is legit."

"Jenson, you're our best. I know. But should I be standing you down from this one?"

Nobody gets stood down. It's a death sentence.

"I wanted you to tell me there was another way."

Westland shakes his head, and I know this is becoming dangerous for me. The wrong answer and it's all over. I go on. "But I see there isn't."

"Okay." He leans back in his chair and grins. "So we're good?"

It's all I can do to not leap across the desk and kill him, punching my way through his face.

I look up at the clock on the wall and concentrate on the second hand moving from the ten to the twelve.

"We're good," I say.

* * * *

Phillips and I are booked into rooms on the same floor as Martenson. Our cover, as always, is that of businessmen here to seal a deal with a Madrid-based firm. We speak to each other in Spanish at the reception desk, going over some minor details of the deal.

We both know the plan. The Madrid team have already bugged the suite where Martenson will stay with his son. Phillips and I will listen in on their arrival and move into the room when they leave. If they don't leave, we wait until they're both asleep and enter via the balcony.

In my room, I set up the equipment and plug in my earphones. It takes two hours for them to arrive; earlier than we'd expected.

"Okay, dude, put your bags over there. Put Jimmy somewhere safe."

I imagine the boy placing a favored teddy bear on his pillow.

Martenson goes on. "You tired?" His accent is a strange mix of Mancunian and Russian.

The kid says, "I'm okay. Can we have pizza, Dad?" As the kid speaks, I look again at his picture.

They talk more about their arrangements for the evening. The boy finds the Disney Channel on TV and keeps telling his dad who all the characters are. "Goofy is silly… Minnie is the girl, she's boring… Mickey is the main one. It's his show."

"I know, pal. I used to watch them when I was little."

"No, you didn't!"

"I *did*." They laugh together, as though they've shared a wonderful joke. I think of Joey, screaming with delight as he began his descent.

After another hour, they go down to the hotel restaurant for pizza. "Can I bring Jimmy with me, Dad?"

"Sure. Why not?"

As soon as they're in the lift, I'm at the door with Phillips keeping watch farther down the corridor. Madrid station have provided key cards which open the doors, so I place it on the reader and enter.

The large suite is still tidy, with a few clothes and toys scattered about. Resting on the pillow of the single bed is a furry brown fox.

Phillips follows me in and, in silence, we take up our positions. I go into the bathroom, step into the bath and pull across the shower curtain. Beyond the bathroom door I can hear Phillips settling himself into the walk-in wardrobe. I take my Glock 46 9mm from the holster and attach the silencer.

In the two weeks since my meeting with Westland, I've thought long and hard about how to approach tonight. I could have insisted Phillips take the kid, but I know they will look closely at me now. They'll have told Phillips to keep an eye on me and ask for a full report when he gets back.

The meeting with Westland was a huge mistake. I exposed myself, showed them I was not the machine they thought I was. If this doesn't go smoothly, they'll dispense with me.

I have to take out the kid and do it well.

I think about the choices I've made during my life, not just with Joey, but all the rest, too. Joining the army, the village in Helmand, the jobs I've done for the ministry. Men and women, good guys and bad guys, who knows? I went down a road and I knew where I was going. I thought I could escape.

Kill enough people and none of them are my responsibility. I'm just processing meat, right?

For a while I believed it.

Now this. A child. There is no escape from this.

I sit down in the bath and try to block it all out. An hour goes by and I think of nothing except little Joey and the cat and the river.

There are sounds outside, Martenson and the child's voice. Happy voices, something about sauce on the kid's face.

The lock beeps and the hotel room door opens. I step out of the bath and listen to them walk past the bathroom. Martenson is saying, "Time for bed, Mister. Big day tomorrow…"

The kid trails behind him and I take the chance. I step out into the corridor and grab him by the neck of his t-shirt. He gives a small yelp and I see his father turn. I pull the kid in, close the door, then lock it. I hold him against me, my hand over his mouth.

Outside, I hear steps. Martenson shouts "No!" Then come the muffled thuds of Phillips's gun.

The boy doesn't know it yet, but his father is dead. There are more heavy sounds as Phillips rearranges Martenson's body. He knows what the police will look for and he'll make no mistakes. After a period of silence, I hear his voice at the door.

It is the first time he has spoken since we were in the hotel lobby. "Jenson. You done in there?"

My hand is still on the boy's mouth and I can feel his tears rolling onto my wrist.

"Just a moment," I say.

I push the child away and turn him around to face me.

I have never seen terror like it. He sobs, "Where's my Daddy?"

Phillips speaks again from the other side of the door. "Jenson, just do it."

As I raise the gun, my hand is shaking.

I try not to look into the kid's eyes, concentrating instead on the section of his forehead which I must blow away.

"Jenson. Do it!"

My gun is dropping a little, so I raise it again to show myself that a decision has been made.

I fire.

The bullet hits the towels shelved above the kid's head.

I put my finger to my lips. He's smart. Even in his state of distress, he understands.

To Phillips I say, "It's done." and flick the lock. I stand back as he comes through the door. When he steps into view, I open up. Four shots, three to his chest, the fourth glancing his left shoulder.

He falls back into the wall of the hallway and slumps to the ground. I follow him out and stand over him, checking the pulse.

With my hand still on Phillips's neck, I say to the kid. "Let's get out of here."

A high-pitched but clear voice responds from behind me. "Jimmy's gonna get you, Mister."

I turn and there is a loud *pop*, then another, then another.

I face him. The boy is stood, feet spread, arms locked, the gun high out in front. The way they teach you at any good gun club.

"Jimmy," I see now, is a .22 calibre Springfield XD, semi-automatic pistol. The leg of his blue jeans is hitched up to reveal a kid-size ankle holster.

Even with the blood running from the side of my neck, I could raise my gun. I could kill him, perhaps save myself. Instead I let the weakness wash over me. I sink to my knees.

I see Joey's face now and I feel, for the first time, the full weight of his loss. My little brother, gone in a moment of, what? Curiosity?

I open my eyes and the sound comes again.

Pop, pop.

Charlie Hughes lives in South London. He began writing suspense, horror and dark psychological short stories three years ago. He's since been published in various magazines and anthologies. His story "The Box" took first prize in the 2016 Ruth Rendell Short Story Competition. "Together" appeared in *Ellery Queen's Mystery Magazine* in March, 2017.

WHALE WATCH

Charles Roland

Delia Fong was gorgeous. Sexy. Wicked little smile, like she knew what you were thinking, and she liked it.

So when she asked me to meet her in Provincetown, I naturally said yes.

The parking situation was atrocious. I gave up looking for curbside spots after ten minutes and left the car by the Pilgrim Monument, paying the attendant fifteen dollars for the privilege and taking my free Provincetown Museum admission, not because I was interested but because it seemed rude not to.

Maybe Delia had a hidden fascination with colonial America that we could explore together.

I've put up with worse.

* * * *

The descent from the Monument to Commercial Street was surprisingly steep. Delia would have called the houses "cute." My sense was that they were old. When I hit the main thoroughfare, I took a long look in both directions. Crowded, even midmorning on a Tuesday, with brunch goers and gallery hoppers and the occasional drag queen.

I walked about a block and a half on Commercial Street, peering into the storefronts and down the little alleyways, and spotted a small gallery up a half a flight of stairs. I opened the door—*ding* went the hanging bell—and stepped inside.

I picked up a business card from a stack on a counter to my left. It said *Pericles* across the top, with an address and phone number in smaller type along the bottom. The image on the card was of a rich blue sea, with a red and white lighthouse nestled in the top right corner.

The card was glossy. It felt expensive.

The next thing I noticed was that everything in the gallery replicated the image on the card. There were large canvases on the walls, smaller framed pieces on the shelves, even pocket-sized tiles propped up on stands in a glass cabinet. All versions of the same scene: blue sea, red and white lighthouse in the top right corner.

"I've been painting them since I was three," said the proprietor, who must have emerged from the back while I was taking in his work. "They were my first words."

He was shirtless, with neatly trimmed facial hair and a belly that protruded over the waistband of his shorts. His skin had a strange quality, as though it had been both tanned dark and somehow bleached.

"Where are you from?" he asked.

"North Carolina," I said.

I'm not, of course. But this is something I say in order to preclude conversation. Telling people on Cape Cod that I'm from North Carolina is a bit like telling them I'm from Macedonia, or Mars. They know the Northeast, and some of them went to college in the Midwest. But with North Carolina, the worst that can happen is someone says, "Chapel Hill?" and I say, "Nope," and that's the end of it. With any luck, when the police ask them, they don't even remember whether I said North Carolina or South Carolina, or Arkansas, maybe? Could it have been Arkansas?

Not this guy, though. He was interested.

"North Carolina? It must be easy to get guns down there, huh?"

What?

"Yeah," I said. "Uh, sure."

"You can just walk into the store and get whatever you need, I bet. How many guns do you have? You have any with you now?"

I was struggling to compose an answer when the bell hanging on the door went *ding* and Joey walked in.

* * * *

Joey and I had been working on the Cape since the start of the season a few months earlier, staying with a friend in Eastham and hitting houses in Wellfleet and Truro while the residents were out biking or at the beach or doing other Cape Cod things.

"Hey," Joey always said, "if the rich guys can go on vacation, then why can't the guys who steal from the rich guys go on vacation, too?"

He had a point.

Joey was always saying stuff like that. Which was funny, if you knew Joey, because he was not really what you'd call a thinker. But every so often he'd come up with something that stuck, like *whale watch*.

It was in Wellfleet, back at the start of the season, and Joey and I had the van with the cable company decal parked in a three-house cul-de-sac a few turns off the main road. Joey was up on the ladder, pretending to noodle around on the utility pole, and it happened that his shirt was a little small, so the bottom third of his midsection was in the breeze.

Now Joey is what you'd call a larger guy. And if there's one thing that Cape Cod vacationers cannot abide, it's fat people.

So this couple came out of one of the houses, all spandex and helmets, walking their bikes beside them. The picture of nicely moneyed, middle-aged health. And the guy took a look up at Joey, and shook his head, and turned to his wife.

"Whale watch," he said, quietly, but loud enough that Joey could hear it. His wife looked up at Joey and shook her head, too, and then they got on their bikes and pedaled away together. Joey, meanwhile, was pretty down in the dumps for a couple of days.

Joey and I revisited that episode two weeks later, in the living room of the couple's house.

They'd gone on one of their bike rides, which by then we knew lasted about three hours. Seeing no other cars parked by the other two houses, Joey and I made our way inside and went to work. After we'd been through the bedrooms and the little office, Joey got the crowbar and we started pulling up the floorboards in the living room.

Cape Cod people—those who aren't renting, anyway—seem to like to nail things under the floorboards. Don't ask me why.

And sure enough, after about ten minutes of irreparable damage to 19th century oak, Joey stuck his hand down and came up with a steel box about the size of a thick book. He held it up and looked at me, and said, "Whale watch!"

Our search was successful. We had spotted the whale.

All the more so after we broke the lock and divided up the stacks of hundred dollar bills.

So when Joey walked into the gallery, looked at me, and raised his eyebrows questioningly, I got the message.

Whale watch?

* * * *

As Joey made his way inside, the proprietor redirected his attention.

"And where are you from?" he asked.

"Uh…" said Joey.

I was already starting to chuckle. Joey didn't thrive under pressure.

"Canada."

Canada was risky. For every person who nodded blankly and changed the subject, there was another who wanted to question you endlessly. What was it like? Was it cold this time of year?

And God forbid you ran into a hockey fan.

"Canada," repeated the proprietor. "Is it easy to get guns up there?"

The look on Joey's face was worth the fifteen-dollar parking.

He stammered his way through an answer, panic in his eyes. The proprietor nodded keenly, eager to continue the conversation.

I was struggling to keep from laughing out loud.

Joey—and I love him for this—is the kind of person who sees the humor in his own foibles. So I took out my phone, held it up as casually as possible, and started to record the scene on video. Joey saw me over the proprietor's shoulder and smiled a little in spite of himself.

My eyes drifted to the canvas next to Joey's panicked face. The image, of course, of a rich blue sea, with a red and white lighthouse in the corner.

Then I caught the price taped to the wall next to the canvas, and I couldn't believe my eyes.

Whale watch!

I lost all interest in Joey's increasingly frantic explanation of Canadian firearm policy, put the phone down on the nearest shelf, and looked for something that might fit in my pocket. The small tiles in the glass cabinet seemed to fit the bill. I glanced over my shoulder to make sure that No-Shirt was still hanging on Joey's every word, and then I flipped one over to check the price.

Six hundred dollars. *Per tile.*

As quickly and silently as I could, I took six of the tiles and slid them into my pockets. Then I walked past Joey and his inquisitive interlocutor, and out the door.

Maybe Provincetown wasn't so terrible after all.

I fast-walked about a block and a half, then ducked behind an outdoor clothing rack in front of an Army-Navy surplus store and pretended to look at tee shirts. Joey caught up with me a minute later.

"You left in a hurry," he said.

"Canada?" I asked.

He shrugged and shook his head, as if to say, *you know how I am.*

And then I saw the shirtless gallery owner over Joey's shoulder, about a block away and closing. Two other men were with him. In their hands, dangling casually at their sides, they held guns.

* * * *

I grabbed Joey and pulled him behind the rack.

"It's the guy. From the gallery. He's got guys with him, and they've got guns."

"He was very interested in guns," Joey said, thoughtfully.

"Yes, he was," I said. "Let's go."

We rounded the side of the Army-Navy store, careful to stay behind the outdoor racks. My car was on the other side of Commercial Street, which we couldn't cross without being seen, so we squeezed by a couple of parked cars and went through the narrow alley to the rear of the building. Fifty feet to our left was the pier, teeming with tourists, tchotchke booths, and what a brochure I'd once read optimistically called "art shacks."

I was skeptical about that last part, but we headed for the pier anyway.

At a booth, Joey spotted a baseball cap with the image of a whale stitched onto it—"whale watch," he said to me, and chuckled—so I waited while he examined it, keeping an eye on the pier's massive parking lot in case No-Shirt and his bodyguards showed up.

Then Joey was next to me again, wearing the whale-themed cap.

"Speaking of whale watch," he said, "what did you get?"

We started walking again, and I fished one of the tiles out of my pocket.

"All of his pictures look like that," Joey said.

I flipped it over so he could see the price. His eyes got wide.

We stopped again so he could take a closer look. Then a voice on the other side of me said, "You ever seen a whale before?"

I turned. The voice belonged to a young guy inside a gray booth, his elbows resting on a dirty counter.

"Uh, yeah, I've seen a whale before."

I had the nature channel. Who was he trying to kid?

He was undeterred. "I mean, in person, right next to you. You ever seen *that* before?"

"No, I guess not," I said.

"Well, you're in luck," said my new friend. "I've got discount whale watch tickets. See?"

He pointed up to the sign above the window. Sure enough: *Discount Whale Watch Tickets.*

I nodded and looked back over at the parking lot.

It was not good.

No-Shirt and his associates were at the edge of the lot, moving toward us. People were giving them a wide berth. It could have been the guns, or it could have been the whole no-shirt thing.

All of a sudden, a whale watch didn't seem like the worst idea.

"How much?" I asked the salesman and had my money on the counter before he finished his reply. I took the tickets, and he pointed toward a dinged-up metal staircase just ahead. Docked at the slip at the bottom of the staircase was the most decrepit-looking boat I had ever seen.

I turned back to the booth, but the window was already closed, and the shades were down.

"Hey, Joey," I said, and pointed toward the decaying boat. "Whale watch."

* * * *

We managed to make it down the stairs and onto the boat without attracting No-Shirt's attention. The clear plastic enclosing the interior portion of the bottom deck was smudged with streaks of mystery grime. The stairs to the top deck were inexplicably sticky. When I leaned on one of the rails around the edge of the deck, it gave about an inch, and I could see the loose screws wiggling in the base.

I would have to keep Joey far away from the railing.

As we waited on the deck, keeping a nervous eye on No-Shirt and his goons, we were approached by an older man with deep wrinkles in his suntanned face. His cheeks boasted thick stubble, and he wore his captain's hat at an angle.

I expected him to say, "Yarrr."

Instead he said, "Should have great weather today. Looking forward to a nice watch for you folks."

He took a look at Joey's new baseball cap.

"I see you've already gotten into the spirit of things," he said.

A handful of other passengers trickled on board over the next few minutes. By the time the mate untied us from the dock, the ship was somewhat less than halfway full.

As we cast off, a tired female voice came across the ship's loudspeakers.

"Hi, folks, and welcome to the *Resilient*. My name's Emma, and I'm going to be your naturalist today."

I looked around for the source of the voice and traced it to a bored-looking blond girl holding a microphone in one hand and thumbing through a smartphone with the other.

"We're going to see lots of great whales today, I bet."

Her enthusiasm was contagious.

"We've got about half an hour's ride out to the feeding ground, so relax, and we'll be with the whales before you know it."

The *thump* when she dropped the microphone in her lap was loud and clear.

I had to admit that the view of Provincetown as we sailed away was striking. Delia would have loved it. Joey, meanwhile, was staring at the open water on the other side of the boat with a look of intense concentration on his face.

"We're not there yet," I said. "No whales here."

Joey looked at me. "I want to be ready," he said.

Fair enough.

Just then a ship approached us heading in the opposite direction. It was a whale watch boat, too, but where ours was falling apart this one was gleaming. It was packed with passengers, and I could hear their naturalist holding forth with gusto as she gestured at large models of various sea life. On the side of the boat it said *Pericles IV*.

Pericles?

The passengers crowding the upper deck of the *Pericles IV* started to wave as we passed, but then they noticed the wretched condition of our boat and seemed to think better of it.

I was starting to feel just a little bit of stubborn pride in the *Resilient*.

"Twelve boats in the Pericles fleet. Time was, we had ten of our own under the Resilient banner. Not anymore, though."

I turned. The weathered captain had posted himself along the rail next to me.

"We stopped into a gallery called Pericles a week or so ago," I said, lying only slightly.

"That's him," said the captain. "Lawrence Pericles. Runs the gallery. Owns the boats. Paints those stupid little lighthouses."

Stupid, maybe, but expensive. I patted the tiles in my pockets.

"He's crooked, too. Everybody knows it. Been taking our boats out of commission one by one since he got into the business five years ago."

His intensity was growing. He stared into my face.

"You wouldn't believe me if I told you. Fuel fires, bombs, even made one of our captains disappear. Anything to drive us under."

The captain must have seen the skepticism in my face.

"Don't believe me, huh? That's all right. We've just got the one boat now. Pretty soon he'll get this one too, and then it'll only be the Pericles fleet sailing out of Provincetown."

The captain shook his head slowly, then walked off.

The bored naturalist came back over the speakers.

"We're just about at the feeding ground, and if you'll look behind the boat, you'll see a school of sharks. Nothing to worry about. They're just looking for a snack or two and hoping to come across some smaller fish."

With the condition of the railing on the upper deck, I thought, the sharks might be in for a bigger snack than they expect.

Just then Joey pointed out toward the horizon.

"Look," he said. "A whale!"

I squinted. Way out in the distance, I could see water shooting up into the air.

"Thar she blows!" said Joey. He was the happiest I'd seen him in weeks.

I decided to go downstairs and see if they had a bar.

The scene on the lower deck was not encouraging. An older woman on one of the benches alongside the enclosed cabin looked to be suffering from seasickness, doubled over and gazing forlornly over the side of the rail. A man lay motionless on the bench next to her. Sleeping, I hoped.

Inside the cabin there were several rows of benches, a concession booth, and a funny smell. I looked around and rested my hand distractedly on the back of one of the benches, where it made contact with a warm, sticky substance that was both gelatinous and gritty.

I wondered if the concession booth sold antibiotics.

I headed for the bathroom behind the last row of benches, not looking forward to what I'd find inside. When I opened the door, I was pleasantly surprised. No stink, no grime, no dead bodies. Just a light-colored countertop, two sinks, a handful of stalls, and a paper towel dispenser.

I was almost disappointed.

I washed my hands thoroughly, dried them, and then balled up the paper and took my best shot at the trashcan at the other end of the counter.

So close!

When I went to retrieve my paper wad, I saw something wedged underneath the counter between the trashcan and the wall. It was... fuzzy. I leaned all the way down and grabbed it.

It was a stuffed whale. White on the bottom and blue on top, with a big head. Cute, really.

Delia would probably love this. No reason to mention that I found it on a bathroom floor.

Hell, Joey would probably love this.

I brushed the whale off and held it up to check for damage. Nothing. I ran my fingers over the plush material, making sure there was nothing at all to indicate its unseemly origins. *Hey, little guy*, I thought, *you might make me very happy later on.*

That's when I heard the beeping. It was quiet, but I heard it. *Beep...*
beep... At regular intervals, like a metronome.

It was coming from the whale.

Whales don't beep.

I put it down and backed away. Then, cautiously, I stepped forward
and picked it back up again.

It was heavy for a stuffed animal.

I started squeezing it lightly, beginning with the tail and moving forward. When I got to the giant head, I felt something solid. I fished my
keys out of my pocket, dug one in right behind the hard plastic eye, and
tore the fabric. When I widened the tear, I could see something solid inside, black, either metal or plastic. I pulled the tear open until half of the
whale's face was gone.

It's amazing how gruesome it feels to dismember a stuffed animal.

Stitched inside the whale's head was a heavy, black, rectangular ob-
ject. Without the plush fabric and stuffing to quiet the sound, I could hear
the beeping clearly. It came from a digital display mounted on the surface
of the device. The red numbers on the display flashed: *57... 56... 55...*
54...

Uh oh.

What had the Captain said about Pericles? *"Been taking our boats*
out of commission one by one... Fuel fires, bombs, even made one of our
captains disappear."

Bombs?

I dropped the whale and ran out of the bathroom and up the stairs to
the upper deck. Joey was still staring at the water. I grabbed his shoulder.

"We have to get off the boat."

He looked up at me. "Where have you been? You missed a humpback
family, right off the side. It's so nice how they stay together."

"Joey, we have to get off. We have to jump off the boat, into the water,
right now. Right now."

"Yeah, right," said Joey. "Shark bait."

He pointed to the water just behind the boat. I could see the fins sticking out of the water, moving leisurely in our wake. The sharks were still
waiting on that snack.

Okay, so we were staying on the boat. I ran back downstairs and into
the bathroom. The whale was still on the counter. The device was still
beeping.

27... 26... 25... 24...

I grabbed the whale and ran back outside. I didn't know where to put it to minimize the damage. Where, on a boat, is the best place for an explosion?

19... 18... 17... 16...

I ran up the stairs to the upper deck. Would Joey know what to do? Does Joey know anything about boats or explosions?

12... 11... 10... 9...

Why did I never learn how to disarm bombs?

7... 6... 5... 4...

I was out of ideas. I took the whale in my right hand, wound up, and threw it as hard as I could off the side of the boat. It hit the water with a splash. I hoped it would sink quickly.

The *boom* was muffled, but I still heard it. The force of the explosion sprayed water upward in a geyser that soaked the *Resilient*'s lower deck.

"Looks like we've got another humpback," said the bored naturalist over the speakers. "That one must have been right next to us. What an experience, huh?"

A handful of the passengers clapped.

I trembled. Joey smiled.

"We know what you did," said the voice behind me.

I wheeled around, expecting—I don't know what I was expecting—Pericles's assassins, maybe?

Instead, I confronted a frowning, middle-aged couple in matching floral shirts.

"We saw what you did," the woman said, "and you should be ashamed."

"Do you know how much work is put into cleaning this feeding ground?" The man asked. "And you just throw your garbage off the boat!"

Now it was her turn. "You're part of the problem," she said, shaking his head. "I wish we had a few more whales, and a few less people like you."

Then they turned and stalked off.

I should've left the bomb right where I found it.

* * * *

Joey spent the rest of the trip on the upper deck watching whales. I spent it laying down on a bench in the cabin with my eyes closed, trying to pretend that I was on dry land and Delia Fong was next to me.

When the naturalist told us that we were returning to Provincetown— "even a great watch like this one has to end, right?"—I figured I'd call Delia and find out if she was in town yet. I patted my pockets. All tiles and no phone. Why no phone?

Then I remembered. I was watching Joey sputter away in Pericles's gallery, and I decided to capture the moment. I was recording the scene when I noticed the price on one of the canvasses, and then... *whale watch!* I grabbed the tiles and hit the road.

My phone was still at Pericles's gallery.

When we docked I took a good look at the pier from the upper deck of the *Resilient*. It took me a few minutes, but I spotted Pericles, sitting at an outdoor bar. He'd disguised himself by putting on a shirt. His guys were with him.

"Here's what I need to you to do," I told Joey. "Remember the guy from the gallery? He's right over there."

Joey looked where I was pointing and nodded.

"Watch him, but don't let him see you. If he starts to look like he's leaving, call that restaurant and ask to speak to Mister Pericles. That's him. I don't care what you say to him but make him stay there."

I paused.

"Tell him it's easy to get guns where you're from. He'll want to hear all about it."

Joey nodded. He may not have been a thinker, but he was dependable.

"I'll be back as soon as I can. Get the number of the restaurant right now so you can call if you need to."

Then I walked down the pier and through the parking lot, careful to stay out of Pericles's sight.

The gallery was open when I got there. I didn't recognize the man behind the counter. I pretended to nose around for a few minutes, looking at the deep blue seas and lighthouses. My phone was still on the shelf, right where I'd left it. I slid it into my pocket next to the tiles and beat a hasty retreat.

On the way back to the pier I took the phone out and looked at the last video I'd taken. I must have put the phone down while it was still recording, because the video was almost thirty minutes long. It recorded until it ran out of memory.

I hit play and watched Joey stammer and fumble. It really was funny. Then the picture went dark. I could still hear, though, which meant I got to find out what Joey said to get himself out of the gallery after I left. It was something about needing to meet his family, who were from an obscure part of Canada. Moose Habitat, I believe, was the town he named.

That nearly made the whole day worth it.

I heard Pericles discovering my theft very shortly after Joey's departure, and I heard him call his guys. Then they left, and there was about fifteen minutes of silence. When they returned, Pericles didn't sound nearly as angry as I'd have thought.

"…always make more. Hell, we can replace them today."

"You got art students making them, boss?"

"Nah, art students are expensive. See these tiles? The guy who did those was delivering pizzas two weeks ago."

I heard his guys laugh.

"I tell them, look, it's just some water and a lighthouse. It's not complicated! Anyone can do it!"

I stopped walking, took one of the tiles out of my pocket, and looked it over.

I will never understand the art world.

I kept walking. On the video, Pericles and his guys were still talking. Then I heard "bomb," and I froze.

"…in a stuffed whale, like the kids buy at the pier."

"That's just perfect. I love it. It's all set?" I heard Pericles ask.

"All set. They'll say the *Resilient* must have had a fuel tank explosion. The shape that boat's in, nobody will look too hard at it."

"It's about time. I'm sick of looking at that old captain. It's like he thinks he's Blackbeard or something. Who's he kidding?"

"Well, in just about an hour he'll be walking the plank."

More laughter. I had to admit, now that I'd met the captain, the Blackbeard thing was kind of funny.

I headed back to the pier as fast as I could.

When I got there, Pericles was still at the bar, and Joey was still watching him closely. The captain was standing outside the ticket booth, talking to the salesman and tallying up receipts. He looked forlorn.

"Hi," I said.

He looked up at me and scowled.

"I have something to show you," I said.

* * * *

An hour later, the police were taking Pericles and his goons away in handcuffs. The captain had shown the video to the authorities and then edited it into small, incriminating segments, which he sent to every media outlet he could think of. Who knew a grumpy old sea dog would be so tech-savvy?

I got a firm handshake and a clap on the shoulder.

"You've saved us, son," said the captain. "And put a very bad man out of business. I've got a feeling the *Resilient* fleet will be back in a big way."

"Great," I said. "Now you can hire a cleaning crew. You could really use one, you know."

The captain squinted at me and frowned. Then a light went on in his eyes, and a smile lit up his face.

"And let's just see him try to sell that lighthouse crap now. Of course a pizza delivery guy could do them. *Anyone* could do them. I bet they're all worth nothing twenty minutes from now. A lot of folks will be feeling pretty stupid about how they spent their money."

I didn't spend any money on my lighthouses, but all of a sudden I felt pretty stupid.

I patted the tiles in my pocket and sighed. They'd make nice coasters, anyway.

* * * *

Delia Fong and I stood on the pier. My hand was wrapped around her hip. She looked up into my eyes. That wicked smile was on her lips. I liked my chances.

I'd been talking to the police when she showed up. They were asking me about the bomb. From this, she got the sense that I'd done something heroic. She felt she needed to take care of me. I did nothing to discourage her.

Like I said, I liked my chances.

"Hey miss! Hey lady!"

The voice came from behind us. Delia turned.

"You ever seen a whale before?"

Delia looked up at me. Her eyes glittered.

"Want to?" she asked.

I looked past her at the young salesman in the *Discount Whale Watch Tickets* booth. I glowered at him. He shrugged.

"No," I said. We walked down the pier toward the parking lot, in the direction of Commercial Street. My hand was still wrapped around her hip.

"Hey," I said. "Have you ever been to the Provincetown Museum?"

✗

Charles Roland lives in an area convenient to several major southern cities. His work has appeared in *Workers Write! Tales from the Casino*, *Mystery Weekly Magazine*, Akashic Books' "Mondays are Murder" series, *Switchblade Magazine*, and more. He can be reached at charlesrolandauthor.com or charlesrolandauthor@gmail.com.

ROAD HOG

James Michael Ullman

This issue's classic reprint originally appeared in Ellery Queen's Mystery Magazine, *November 1957.*

Barlow cursed and slammed his foot down on the brake pedal, at the same time turning the wheel sharply. Tires screamed and his car jerked to a halt.

Why, the guy would have run right into him if Barlow hadn't stopped! Made a left turn smack into Barlow's path!

Slowly, the other car continued its turn. Barlow's window was down. As the other car, an old green sedan, pulled alongside headed in the opposite direction, Barlow stuck his head out.

"Careful, dear," his wife Evelyn cautioned.

But Barlow glared at the other driver, a stupid-faced, immense man with dark brows and mammoth shoulders encased in a leather jacket. The other driver was alone. His window was also down.

"You road hog," Barlow shouted. "You drive like a crazy man. You made that turn right in front of me. Didn't you see me coming? You ought to be in an asylum instead of driving a car on the city streets!"

The other car slowed down, as though the big driver intended to stop and reply. But Barlow angrily pulled his head in, shoved his own car into first, and stepped on the gas. As he sped away, Barlow looked in the rearview mirror and saw that the other car had come to a stop, and that the other driver was looking back at him.

"Guys like that," Barlow said tensely, eyes straight ahead, "got to be told off now and then. They'll give any knucklehead a license to drive these days."

"You were driving pretty fast yourself, dear," his wife pointed out. "This isn't a one-way street, you know."

"He saw me coming," Barlow replied irritably. "He had no call to make a turn that way. All he had to do was wait a second and let me go by."

His wife shrugged and looked away.

"All right," she sighed. "But I still don't think you should shout at other drivers. One day you'll get us into trouble."

* * * *

Barlow was involved in another traffic incident a few minutes later. It happened at a stoplight to an intersection a half block from the cloverleaf to the superhighway. Barlow intended to take the superhighway out of the city.

The light was red. Barlow's car was in the first rank. His car was in gear and as the red snapped to yellow, Barlow stepped on the accelerator and his car jolted forward. But a delivery truck, trying to make the yellow light on the cross street before the light turned red, loomed unexpectedly before him. Barlow had to screech to a stop part-way through the intersection in order to avoid a collision.

Barlow gazed with hatred at the disappearing delivery truck. He shoved the gear back into first and clomped down hard on the accelerator, starting the car again with a squeal of tires.

"Some people," he muttered. "Probably some punk kid driving that truck. Put a kid in a truck that doesn't belong to him and he drives like a maniac."

"You're going pretty fast," his wife said. "The Nortons aren't expecting us until two. We've got plenty of time."

"Not on a Sunday," Barlow replied grimly. His car was now in a line turning into the cloverleaf and Barlow had to slow down. Steering the car with one hand, he put a cigarette in his mouth, ignited it with the dashboard lighter, and puffed intently. They arrived at the expressway and Barlow cut sharply into traffic, forcing another car to veer to an outside lane.

"Every screwball and his cousin are out on the road on Sunday," Barlow went on authoritatively. "All the goofs who never drive a car during the week. They pile the kids into the car on Sunday and go rubbernecking around, cluttering up every highway. Those people don't know how to drive on modern turnpikes. They drive slow in the fast lanes and fast in the slow ones. Here, see what I mean? This idiot ahead of me."

Barlow had been maneuvering from lane to lane in order to pass the slower drivers. He was in the next-to-fastest lane now but was trapped behind a slow-moving sedan. Through the rear window of the car ahead two little girls peered wonderingly at him. The couple in the front seat were obviously their parents.

"This guy is a jerk," Barlow pronounced. "At the speed he's going, he has no right to be in this lane. He ought to be over in the slow lane—

cripes!"

Barlow accelerated a little and pulled to within a few feet of the car ahead, trying to force the other driver to increase speed. He followed the other car that way for about a quarter of a mile, but the other driver refused to change his plodding pace.

"You'd think," Barlow said sarcastically, "that he'd catch on and get out of the way. But no, not him—oh, no!"

Barlow tooted his horn—a long, insistent blast. The little girls in the rear window waved gaily.

"Oh, brother," Barlow exclaimed. "I give up!"

Barlow flopped back in his seat, holding the steering wheel lightly with the fingers of his left hand. He slowed to the point where the car that had been abreast of him on the left got far enough ahead for Barlow to cut out suddenly into the left lane, and then Barlow stepped on the gas.

* * * *

"Dear," his wife said tentatively.

"What is it?" Barlow asked with a show of irritation. He was trapped again behind another slow car. They had been on the superhighway for nearly half an hour now, one of hundreds of cars moving swiftly along the big white track.

"That car that just went by—the one up ahead on the right. That man was in it."

"What man?"

"The man you shouted at. You know, the man who made the turn in front of you back on Evergreen Street."

Barlow glanced briefly in the direction his wife had indicated. Yes, there was an old green sedan resembling the car that had made the turn; but Barlow couldn't be sure.

"I doubt it," he said. "The guy wasn't going in our direction."

"He could have turned around and followed us," his wife said. "And I'm *sure* that's the man. He stared at us as he went by. He was a very big man in a leather jacket and he looked sort of sullen. He didn't look right to me."

"You're imagining things," Barlow replied. He experienced a tinge of concern himself, but then reasoned that if it really was the man, it was only coincidence. A lot of cars traveled the superhighway on Sunday afternoon. There would be no reason why the man in the leather jacket shouldn't travel it, too.

"I didn't like that man," Evelyn Barlow said. "He looked mighty queer to me. You shouldn't have shouted at him. And you shouldn't have called him crazy."

"Don't be silly," Barlow said. He saw an opening to his left and cut sharply into the fast lane. Then he relaxed and bore down on the gas pedal. The drivers ahead of him in this lane knew their stuff, all right. They were all barreling along at about seventy.

"We're passing him," his wife said.

"Where?"

"Over there—two lanes over."

Barlow craned his head for a quick glance but didn't see much. Just that it was an old green sedan. He couldn't get a glimpse of the driver.

Barlow turned his head back to face the road.

"Well, he's behind us now," he said. "Traffic will thin out after the next big turnoff. Whoever the guy is, we'll leave him far behind. That old heap of his will never catch up with us."

Evelyn Barlow had turned in her seat and was peering back.

"He's still there," she reported. "It looks as if he's changing lanes. He's moving out into our lane—yes, there he is. He's in our lane now. I can't see him any more—but he's in our lane."

"Stop that," Barlow commanded. "Turn around and forget that old car. The chances are a million to one against it being the same man."

"But he *stared* at us."

"Nonsense!"

"I wish the Nortons didn't live so far out," his wife continued. "I wish they lived some place closer where there are lights and people and things. I don't like those little side roads out where the Nortons live."

"Stop talking like a schoolgirl," Barlow said. "Relax and try to enjoy yourself."

* * * *

The road where Barlow turned off was nearly at the end of the expressway. Traffic had thinned considerably at this point. As Barlow veered off the expressway and slowed for the cloverleaf, his wife, despite Barlow's admonition, turned again and looked back.

"Well," Barlow asked with mock jocularity, "do you still see our mysterious friend?"

"I'm not sure."

"Well, I'm sure," Barlow said. "In the first place, it probably isn't the same man. In the second place, if it is the man, he probably turned off before now. And in the third place, if he didn't turn off, he couldn't have kept up with us. I was going nearly eighty that last stretch."

They stopped for a red light at the end of the cloverleaf. Except for a restaurant and a motel the countryside was desolate. Barlow drummed his fingers impatiently on the steering wheel.

"Ridiculous," he muttered. "Putting a traffic signal out here in the middle of nowhere. They ought to have a stop sign, that's enough." The light turned green. Barlow pulled away.

"That Ed Norton," Barlow said. "I suppose he'll want to serve martinis before dinner. Ever watch Ed Norton make a martini? It's a joke. He uses at least half vermouth. Me, I'm sticking to bourbon on the rocks all afternoon."

"Don't drink too much," his wife advised. "Remember we have a long drive home."

"Don't you worry about me."

"I think it would be nice, dear, if we left a little earlier this time. Before dark."

"Are you kidding? Four times a year or so we see Ed and Marie Norton and you want to drop in and eat Marie's dinner and then say goodbye! Why, the Nortons used to be our best friends when we lived on Montgomery Street. We can't be rude. You know Ed. He'll want to play poker after dinner, and Marie always fixes a late snack. Anyhow, I dropped six bucks the last time we had a session and I intend to win it back."

They had been driving rapidly up a long, gentle slope. As they neared the crest, Barlow glanced into his rear-view mirror. Far behind him another car had turned off the expressway and was heading in the same direction. It might be an old green sedan, but at this distance Barlow couldn't be sure. Barlow's car topped the hill. He pushed his right foot farther down on the gas pedal.

"You're going too fast for this narrow little road," his wife said.

"Don't want to be late," Barlow muttered.

* * * *

Barlow had his hat and coat on, and a glass in his hand.

"Here's one for the road," he said. He tipped the glass, drained it, and set it down on a coffee table. "It's been great, Ed. We want you and Marie to come see us next month—after we get the new carpeting. Things are in a mess right now."

They shook hands all around. Ed and Marie Norton walked out to the car with the Barlows. It was dark and even with the porch light on Barlow stumbled once or twice.

"Take it easy going back," Norton said. "They're doing a lot of construction on the stretch two miles up the road. There's a pretty steep drop on the left that doesn't have any guard rail."

"Don't worry," Barlow said. "I know the road by heart."

He got in on the driver's side and Ed Norton opened the other door for Mrs. Barlow. The doors slammed shut. Barlow switched on the ignition and started the motor.

"Be seeing you," Barlow called. "Ed, I'll give you a ring next week. And thanks for letting me win my money back."

"So long."

"Goodbye," Evelyn Barlow said.

Barlow's car lurched slowly down the driveway and into the road, the headlights cutting through the darkness.

"It's pretty late," his wife said. "After ten."

"Probably midnight before we get home. It's chilly."

"Close the window then."

They turned a corner and Norton's house was out of sight. Occasionally they passed other houses but for long stretches on this winding road they saw no lights at all. Barlow was driving at about forty.

"That construction area comes up about now," Barlow said. They approached another turn and Barlow took his foot off the gas pedal and gradually slowed down.

But as they started into the turn another pair of headlights snapped on almost in front of them. Another car came bounding out of a side road, forcing Barlow to turn his wheel and brake hard. Barlow's wife screamed. Barlow shouted in incoherent rage and held tight to the wheel, finally stopping the car on the shoulder of the road. The other car had pulled up beside him.

Barlow put his head out the window.

"You madman," he raged. "What in hell do you think you're doing?" No reply came from the other car. As Barlow's eyes became accustomed to the dark he noticed that it was an old car. An old sedan. Green, maybe.

Then the other car's door opened. A stolid, massive figure stepped out—a man in a leather jacket...

* * * *

The state trooper was down on his knees, examining the tire marks with his flashlight. Below him, on the ledge of rocks, a small group of men had gathered about the wreckage of what had been Barlow's car. They were extricating the bodies.

"He wasn't going fast at all," the trooper mused. "Wonder what made him go clean off the road that way?"

"We'll never know," said a sheriff's deputy standing beside him. "Funny thing. They both had broken backs. Broken in the same way. Sort of freak accident. I don't quite see how it could have happened."

The trooper rose and stretched. He rubbed the back of his head.

"You know," he said, "there was one just like it out by Hadley Road last spring. Guy driving alone at night went smack into a brick wall for no good reason. He had a busted back, too, and I couldn't figure out how he got it. Then three weeks ago, another guy—he was alone at night too. Found his car upside-down in a ditch by the canal with him dead the same as those two down there. Almost as if some very big man put them across his knee and snapped their spines. But it must be coincidence. What else could it be?"